ROMANCE

# A RUMOURED ENGAGEMENT

# A RUMOURED ENGAGEMENT

BY
CATHERINE GEORGE

MILLS & BOON®

First published in Great Britain 1997
Large Print edition 1998
Harlequin Mills & Boon Limited,
Eton House, 18-24 Paradise Road,
Richmond, Surrey TW9 1SR

© Catherine George 1997

ISBN 0 263 15585 4

Set in Times Roman
16-9806-48415 C16½-17½

Printed and bound in Great Britain
by Antony Rowe Ltd, Chippenham, Wiltshire

# CHAPTER ONE

THE bright Tuscan sunlight was almost gone. When it became too dark to read Saskia let her book fall gently to the flagged floor, turned on the 'hot' tap with her toe until the water was warm enough, and sank back in surroundings picturesque enough to tempt any lingerer. The crimson roll-top art nouveau bath had a white interior and white claw feet, its eighteen-nineties elegance harmonising well with the ancient stone walls of the bathroom. Piles of white crimson-bordered towels lay near the bath on a gilt and wicker stool, and on the far wall a large, dim mirror in an ornate gilt frame reflected the last glow of sunset.

Saskia roused herself eventually to wash her hair, kneeling with the spray attachment turned on her head until the water ran clear, then stood up, thrusting the streaming hair from her face. And froze, arm upraised, as the door opened and a man stopped dead on the thresh-

5

old, as though he'd walked into glass. He stared in shock for a split second, muttered an appalled apology and slammed the door shut. Heart hammering, Saskia let out a long, shaky breath, and leapt from the bath to wrap herself in a towelling robe. She swathed a towel turban-wise round her hair, then breathed in, squared her shoulders and sallied forth to confront the intruder.

He was outside on the terrace, tall and loose-limbed in jeans and a thin cotton shirt, tawny hair lit by the last glow of sunset, familiar in every detail. He turned from contemplation of the landscape to greet her with the wry, lop-sided smile which most women, other than Saskia, found so irresistible.

'Hello, little sister. I apologise humbly. I had no idea you were here.'

'Likewise.' Saskia eyed him militantly. 'Mother didn't say you were in the neighbour-hood.'

'Or you'd have given Tuscany a wide berth?'

'Not at all,' she retorted. 'You frightened me out of my wits, that's all. I thought you were an intruder.'

'Which I am, of course. I should have checked with Marina.' He looked over her shoulder into the large sparsely furnished room. 'I take it Lawford is with you?'

'No, he's not.'

'No?' He raised a quizzical eyebrow. 'I thought you two were more or less joined at the hip these days. During my last visit to Oxford, Marina seemed to think you'd found Mr Right at last.'

'At *last*?' Her eyes glittered coldly.

He leaned on one of the archways, arms folded. 'You can't deny an impressively long line of hopeful contenders for your fair hand in the past, Sassy. But I heard Francis Lawford was thought to be the lucky man.'

'Don't be sarcastic,' she snapped.

His green eyes opened in mock surprise. 'I meant it quite literally, little sister. The man you choose will be fortunate indeed.'

Saskia eyed him suspiciously. 'I never know when you're being serious, Lucius Armytage.'

'I know,' he agreed affably. 'All part of the Armytage charm. Now, before you cast me out into the night, would you mind very much if I had the bath I was after earlier on?'

'You've as much right to a bath and bed here as me,' she said grudgingly. Then, abruptly, as much to her own surprise as his, offered to provide supper. 'I've made some pasta. There's enough for two. You can share it, if you like.'

He stared at her blankly for a moment, then smiled. 'I'd like that very much, Sass— Saskia,' he amended hurriedly at her scowl. 'Give me half an hour to wash off the picturesque dust of Tuscany and I'll be the perfect supper guest.' He sketched a mocking bow. 'And provide the obligatory bottle, of course. I left a fair selection here on my last visit.'

Saskia shrugged. 'It's a pretty ordinary meal, oh, Master of Wine. Not fit for your finest Barolo, or whatever.'

'I'm sure I'll find something appropriate.' He paused in the doorway. 'Now I come to think of it, we've never shared a meal alone together before, little sister. Which calls for something special to mark the occasion.'

Saskia watched him go, frowning, then took off the towel and shook out her hair, gazing at the stars piercing the twilight sky. She had run away to the Villa Rosa to lick her wounds in private. But after three days of her own undiluted company she found she quite welcomed the prospect of a guest for dinner. Even in the shape of Luke Armytage.

In her uncluttered bedroom on the upper floor, where pale curtains moved gently at the open window, Saskia dried her hair, brushing it into the chin-length bell-like shape she'd paid a small fortune for the week before in London. Her departure had been hurried, with only a large canvas hold-all for luggage, which meant that her choice of clothes was limited. And because Luke had a maddening habit of looking just right at all times, Saskia discarded the jeans and sweatshirt she'd had ready in favour of a short, clinging dress in dark brown jersey with a plunging V-shaped neckline.

After three long days spent in Tuscan sunshine her olive skin was the colour of honey, and to show off her tan she thrust the sleeves up to her elbows, slid her bare feet into gilt thonged sandals, and added a few deft touches to her eyes and lips. When she went downstairs Luke was waiting for her on the terrace, dressed in pale trousers and a yellow shirt, his wet hair slicked back. Two large glasses and an opened bottle of wine waited on one of the tables.

'I thought we might have some of this beforehand,' he said, half filling the glasses.

Saskia took one from him with a word of thanks. 'What shall we drink to?'

'To us,' he said promptly, and swirled the wine in his glass, sniffing deeply. 'Not bad,' he pronounced, after tasting it.

She copied the process mockingly, took in a little air with the wine, and savoured the taste on her tongue. 'Delicious. Not that I'm an expert like you. What is it?'

'You mentioned pasta, which is what I meant to cook for myself tonight, so I looked out a local table wine. This one's particularly good—note the fresh crimson tint. How would you describe the flavour?'

Saskia took another mouthful and waited for the aftertaste, which lingered long enough to tell her the wine was a good one. 'Cherries?'

Luke nodded. 'Clever girl. Juicy, bitter cherries, at that.' He raised his glass again. 'To my good fortune.'

'You've run something really special to earth today?'

'In a way.' He gave her a leisurely top-to-toe inspection. 'I meant I'm pleased to have an unexpected companion for dinner. And you look very special indeed, Sassy. Am I allowed to pay you compliments?'

'The "special" part's all right,' she retorted, 'but not the name.'

'All right, Saskia. I won't tease.' He held out the bottle, but she shook her head.

'I'll leave it until we eat. Otherwise you'd have to cook the dinner.'

'I can, easily,' he assured her.

'I know. You can do everything,' she said, resigned. 'Tonight, however, you'll have to put up with my cuisine.'

'Gladly!'

She eyed him suspiciously. 'You're being very nice to me tonight, Luke. Why?'

'Does there have to be a reason?'

She looked away. 'I thought my mother might have said something.'

He shook his head. 'I haven't spoken to Marina for some time. I've been on my usual treasure hunt. I only hope the business isn't grinding to a halt in my absence.'

Lucius Armytage was a wine merchant, with two London-based shops and a mail-order service, all of them specialising in quality wines for the connoisseur. Although only in his mid thirties, he was a Master of Wine, a successful businessman, and the author of a book dedicated to bringing the pleasure of wine to a wider audience. And in the ten years since his father had married her mother he had always managed to rouse resentment in Saskia Ford.

Tonight, it seemed, despite the embarrassing incident earlier, Luke was favouring her with the easy charm he normally reserved for the rest of her sex.

'You can stay here and watch the stars come out,' she said, getting up. 'Or you can come and watch while I put the meal together.'

Luke got up at once, and collected the glasses and wine. 'That's no choice, little sister.'

In the kitchen Saskia put a pan of sauce on to heat, and without being asked Luke put knives and forks on the table, found checked cotton napkins and talked easily of his travels in his constant search for quality wine to sell in his shops.

'I've been in Piedmont—or Piemonte, whichever you like. Magnificent food, and wine to match.'

'It must be a wonderful thing to have a satisfying job which takes you to such beautiful places,' she said enviously, and plunged fresh ribbons of pasta into a pot of boiling water.

'Don't you enjoy your job?' he said, surprised. 'I thought life on the trading floor of your smart bank was the ultimate buzz.'

'It was, once.' Saskia shrugged. 'Lately I've lost the taste for it. But I've got a mortgage to pay off, and so on, so I suppose I just have to stick at it. I'm not a City trader with a high salary, remember. I've been Charles Harrison's PA for so long he takes me for granted, keeps delegating more and more to me—but enough of that. This is nearly ready.'

They sat down to steaming plates of pasta bathed in a tomato sauce perfumed with garlic and basil, and rich with mussels and prawns.

'Ah,' said Luke, sniffing the air with reverence as he poured the wine. 'Marina's special sauce.' He shot a look at Saskia. 'Did you make this?'

'Of course. I made the pasta, too.'

They ate without talking for a while—Saskia's hunger, for the first time in days, matching that of her unexpected visitor.

Luke paused to cut hunks off the loaf which lay nearby on a board. 'Want some of this to mop up?'

Saskia nodded, wiping the bread round her plate greedily until the last drop was gone, something she would never have done in company with Francis.

'Were you expecting company tonight?' Luke asked curiously when their plates were empty.

'No.'

'Then how did you have this ready and waiting?'

'I made the basic sauce and the pasta yesterday, but I haven't been feeling very hungry lately, so I left it for today and added the mussels and prawns. Which was lucky for you. Your timing was impeccable.' She got up to take the plates. 'There's some *pecorino* in the fridge.'

'Perfect.' Luke watched her as she set the cheese and a bowl of peaches on the table. 'How long have you been here?'

'Three days.'

'How long are you staying?'

'Eleven more, unless I get bored with my own company.' Saskia eyed him with sudden hostility. 'Why? Am I in your way?'

Luke shook his head, and cut another slice of bread to eat with his cheese. 'It's the other way round, surely? You were here first.' His eyes met hers. 'Did you know that Marina gave me a key to this place years ago? It's a boon to me on my travels. I get heartily fed up with hotels.'

'I knew you used it occasionally, of course.' A faint, wry smile touched the corners of her mouth. 'I didn't give you a thought on my headlong rush here, I'm afraid.'

'Or at any other time,' he said dryly, and began peeling a peach with precision, his eyes fixed on the task. 'Am I allowed to ask *why* you rushed?'

Saskia shrugged. 'I suppose so. Though it's not very interesting. I was going to spend my holiday in a very different way. But fate had a trick up her sleeve.'

Luke leaned forward and laid the peach on her plate. 'I assume this is something to do with Francis Lawford?'

'Yes.'

'Then if he's hurt you in some way I imagine you hold me responsible.'

Saskia stared at him. 'Why on earth should I do that?'

'I introduced him to you.' Luke's long, flexible mouth went down at the corners. 'He was damned persistent about it. You remember the occasion?'

Saskia nodded. Her mother and stepfather had persuaded her to go with them to a wine tasting at one of Luke's shops. And Francis

Lawford, development director of a successful restaurant group, had been among the other guests. He fancied himself as something of a connoisseur, and was a regular customer at Armytage Wines, both for himself and for the restaurant chain. The rest, she thought morosely, was history. Past history now.

'Until recently I was very grateful for the introduction,' she assured Luke. 'But I don't want to talk about that right now. The dinner wasn't bad, and the wine was wonderful. I don't want to ruin a pleasant evening.' Which was true, she realised, with faint surprise. The evening so far had been far more pleasant than expected.

Luke laughed. 'I'd take that as more of a compliment if you didn't look so astonished about it.'

Saskia smiled suddenly, and he nodded in approval.

'That's better. The first real smile since I arrived.'

'Since I arrived, too,' she said lightly. 'Let me clear this away, then we'll have coffee on the terrace.'

'Right.' Luke got up and went over to one of the floor-to-ceiling cupboards. 'There should be some Vin Santo in here to drink with it.'

'Don't you ever think of anything but wine?' she said, laughing.

He turned mocking eyes on her. 'Indeed I do. But I won't shock you by giving details of my private life! Besides, Vin Santo is regarded here as the wine of friendship. It might help to stop us fighting.' He sobered, looking at her searchingly, then turned back to the cupboard. 'Is Marina perfectly happy about your solitary holiday?'

'Not perfectly, no. What are you looking for?'

'Eureka,' he said in triumph, and returned to the table with a bottle of Vin Santo and a packet of *santucci*—hard little almond biscuits—to eat with it. He filled two small glasses, and dipped one of the biscuits into his own. 'Go on. When in Rome, and all that.'

Saskia dipped a biscuit, and nibbled. 'I hope I can sleep after all this.'

'Has sleep been difficult lately?'

'Yes.'

There was silence for a moment. Then Luke stretched out a hand and touched hers very fleetingly. 'Problems, Sassy?'

She removed her hand, and turned away to the coffee pot on the stove. 'Nothing I won't solve. In time.'

'In other words, Mind your own business, Armytage.'

Saskia shook her head. 'I didn't mean that at all. It's just hard to admit that I've been a fool.'

'Over Lawford?'

'Yes.'

Luke contemplated her thoughtfully. 'Is there anything I can do? In my capacity as brother I could go and have a word with him for you, if you like.'

'In which case you might lose his order. I gather it's pretty substantial. And in any case you're not my brother.'

'I'm your stepbrother.'

'Just because my mother married your father it doesn't mean *we're* related, Lucius Armytage,' she retorted.

Luke's eyes frosted over. 'No. You've always made that very plain.' He drained his glass and stood up. 'The wine didn't work after all. Don't bother about coffee, I'm for bed—'

'Please don't go yet,' said Saskia urgently. 'I'm sorry, Luke. I didn't mean to snap.' She managed a smile. 'I'm actually rather tired of my own company. We could play some music, or just count the stars. We don't have to talk.'

He looked at her in silence for a moment, then shrugged. 'We can talk for a while, if that's what you want.'

Outside, under the pergola, they sat in silence in the starlit darkness at first, then began talking about their respective parents, and the twins, and Saskia's job as PA to the head of capital markets in one of the City's merchant banks.

'I'm thinking of making a move,' she said, with a sigh. 'Orchestrating the constant changes in my boss's schedule is quite a challenge. Of course I like the client contact and the project work. And the bank is a prestigious one—looks good on my CV. But the past few days on my own here have given me time to think, take stock. Here in Tuscany the City seems like something on another planet.' She smiled. 'Of course, when I get back home I'll probably be glad of the hustle and bustle. But at the moment I hate the thought of it.'

Luke's wicker chair creaked as he stretched out his long legs. 'I'm fortunate, I suppose. My way of earning my daily bread is unfailingly interesting—to me, anyway—not least because I travel regularly in pleasant places.'

'But everything always has gone smoothly for you, Luke.'

'Not entirely.' He paused. 'I wasn't very happy when my parents divorced, believe me.'

Saskia bit her lip. 'I'm sorry. I didn't think. How old were you when they parted? Thirteen, fourteen?'

'Fifteen. Not quite grown up. In fact still young enough to bawl like a baby the night my mother told me she was going to live in America with Joe Harley. I could spend my holidays in California with them, she assured me, and we could talk on the phone all the time, and write to each other regularly. None of which was much comfort to me at the time.'

Saskia sat very still, listening intently. Luke had never said a word on this particular subject before.

'In the end,' Luke went on, 'I even gained in some ways. I owe my interest in wine to Joe. He was always very good to me. I spent a lot of holidays helping out in his vineyards in Napa Valley, learning about New World viticulture almost by osmosis.'

'But you lived with your father.'

'Until I could afford a place of my own, yes. Dad had some idea about selling the house in Oxford at first, but I think he kept it on so I wouldn't have too many changes to cope with at once. And now he's glad he did, of course.' He chuckled. 'Funny, really. My mother couldn't cope with the academic life. Marriage to an Oxford don wasn't her scene at all. Yet Marina seems to thrive on it. But I've often wondered if she minded moving into what was virtually another woman's home.'

'Mother and I lived in a cramped little flat over her dress shop, Luke, so she adored the house from the first. Besides, she made some changes once we moved in. Even more when the boys were born.' She paused. 'How did you feel when the twins arrived?'

Luke laughed. 'Astonished, at first. But who could resist that pair of charmers? My father was as pleased as Punch. I was happy for him. He spent ten lonely years on his own before he met your mother, remember. She gave him a new lease of life.' He turned to look at her. 'Your father died before you were born, I know. While we're on the subject, how did you shape up to the thought of a stepfather?'

Saskia was quiet for a moment. 'At first,' she said slowly, 'I was afraid and miserable, sure Sam would come between Mother and me. But I soon got over that once I knew him better. He's always been kindness itself to me.'

'The only fly in the ointment, then, was me.'

Saskia had been fifteen, and Luke ten years older when Samuel Armytage had married Marina Ford. Saskia had been prickly and full of illogical resentment for the good-looking, energetic young man, who had already opened the first of his shops and owned a smart car and a flat in Parsons Green.

'You were so perfect, Lucius Armytage, and so superior and horribly pleased with yourself. You always had some gorgeous, slender sexpot in tow, while I was a seething mass of teenage angst with puppy fat, spots on my face and braces on my teeth. How I loathed you!'

'Don't I know it?' he said with feeling. 'I used to time my visits home for when you weren't around.'

'Don't think I didn't notice!'

He laughed. 'I hope I've changed a bit since then. *You* certainly have. Our paths haven't crossed for a while lately, but I hear the news from Dad and Marina. They seemed rather relieved that you'd stopped changing the boyfriend every five minutes and settled on one, at last.'

'Wrong one, as it happens,' she said lightly.

'Want to talk about it?'

'No, thanks. You don't want a tearful woman on your hands at this time of night.'

'Hurt badly, Sassy?'

His tone was so unexpectedly tender her throat thickened.

'Hopping mad, rather than hurt,' she said gruffly. 'With myself, for being such a fool. Mortifying. I honestly thought I had better judgement.'

'I meant what I said about having a word with Lawford,' he said casually, getting to his feet. 'Or whatever you prefer in the way of chastisement. I object to my relatives getting hurt.'

'But we're not really relatives, Luke.'

'How would you describe us, then?'

'Connections?'

'Too remote. As far as Lawford's concerned you're my stepsister.' His smile was even more crooked than usual. 'I reserve the right to come the heavy brother if he's caused you lasting damage, Saskia.'

'The damage is to my pride only—and very temporary. But thank you for the thought. It's very—sweet of you.'

Luke chuckled. 'That's a first. No one's ever called me sweet before.'

'Not even Zoë?'

'Definitely not Zoë. You're out of touch. That's been over some time.'

Something Saskia knew perfectly well. 'Really? Who's the current lady, then?'

'There isn't one. I've been too busy.' Luke took the tray from her. 'I'll see to these if you're tired.'

'How domesticated,' she mocked, and followed him through the living room and out into the kitchen.

'We single chaps have to be these days.'

'Doesn't some kind lady wait on you hand and foot in your new house?'

Under the bright overhead light Luke gave her a sardonic look as he put the cups in the sink. 'I have a cleaner, yes, whom I cherish because she's large, cheerful, efficient and a doting grandma. As long as I exclaim over photographs of her brood she's willing to "do" for me a couple of hours twice a week. Otherwise I cope unaided.'

'And cope brilliantly, of course.'

'Of course.'

Saskia shook her head, smiling, then yawned suddenly. 'Sorry.'

'Don't be. Perhaps you'll sleep better to-night.'

'I hope so. Goodnight, Luke.'

'Goodnight, little sister. I'll just sit on the terrace a while longer.'

Which was rather tactful of him, thought Saskia as she made preparations for the night. It saved bumping into him again tonight in awkward circumstances. She brushed her teeth vigorously, her cheeks burning. All evening she'd done her best to forget the earlier confrontation here in the bathroom. And Luke, somewhat to her surprise, had behaved as though their first meeting had been on the terrace. Which was unusual. His dealings with her normally held more than a tinge of mockery. Perhaps he'd been just as embarrassed as she was, of course. Or was being tactful because he was sorry for her—not a thought which pleased. She hated the thought of pity from Luke, or from anyone else.

Saskia stared at her flushed reflection, furious with herself now for spending so much money on her hair to please Francis. The hairdresser had added fine threads of gold here and there to highlight the tawny brown, and it looked good. But somehow it also emphasised the fact that she was alone here in Italy, instead of in London with Francis. Not that she was alone tonight. Despite their past lack of rapport she had been surprisingly glad of Luke's company after the initial fright. She had begun to be tired of her own company. She would even miss him when he went on his way in the morning.

# CHAPTER TWO

IN THE morning, however, Saskia got up to find Luke sitting at the breakfast table with a pot of coffee in front of him, obviously in no hurry to go anywhere.

'Good morning,' she said, yawning.

'Good morning, Sassy. Sleep well?'

She nodded. 'Actually, I did. My sleepless nights finally caught up with me.'

Luke raised an eyebrow. 'Or maybe you were more relaxed with company in the house.'

Saskia helped herself to coffee from the pot and sat down. 'I'm not nervous on my own, Luke.' She looked at him squarely. 'What exactly are your plans? Is my presence here a problem?'

He returned the look in silence for a moment, then shrugged. 'I admit I'd intended staying here for a few days. I should have checked with Marina. But not to worry; I'll find a hotel.'

She drank some of her coffee. 'You don't have to do that,' she said, after a while. 'I'm sure we can manage to occupy the same house for a few days without coming to blows. Especially if you intend to be out every day.'

'I can arrange to be out every evening as well,' he said dryly, 'if you'd prefer.'

Saskia could well imagine it. Luke was the sort of man who had friends everywhere. And not all of them female, she allowed, with justice.

'It makes no difference to me either way,' she said, deliberately indifferent. 'Want some breakfast? No bacon and egg, though—just fruit, yoghurt and a couple of yesterday's rolls I could heat up. I need to do some shopping.'

'I could run you somewhere, if you like,' he offered.

She shook her head. 'No, thanks. I'll walk to the village later.'

Luke jumped to his feet. 'As you like. If you'll excuse me I'll take a shower. I skipped one earlier, in case I woke you.'

'I'll have breakfast ready by the time you are, then.'

He shook his head. 'Don't bother, Saskia. I'll get something on my travels.' He strode from the room without looking at her, and she stared after him, biting her lip.

She had offended him again. Which was by no means the first time. But this time, for once, she hadn't intended to. On the rare occasions they spent time in each other's company these days they were usually in Oxford, with Sam and Marina, and made an effort to remain civil. Not, conceded Saskia with sudden honesty, that Luke was ever uncivil. She was the culprit. Due to an in-house gym at the bank and a determinedly healthy diet her skin was good these days, and while she would never be thin she was no longer overweight. Nevertheless, the moment she was in Luke's company some secret part of her instantly reverted to the plump, hostile teenager of their first meeting.

Saskia switched the oven on, set out butter, fruit and some cartons of yoghurt, made a fresh pot of coffee, then went out to sit on the terrace to lie in wait for Luke, in case he intended taking off without saying goodbye. She heard him leave the bathroom, then a minute or two later he came out on the terrace, wearing well-cut jeans and a white shirt, a lightweight jacket over his arm. But there was no suitcase in evidence, she noted, brightening.

'I'm off, then, Saskia,' he said briskly.

'If you've got time, please stay and have breakfast first,' she said. 'I obviously put my foot in it again just now. I really didn't mean to.'

Luke looked down at her, eyes narrowed, then he shrugged and laid his jacket down on one of the wicker chairs. 'All right.'

They ate yoghurt and peaches in silence, then Saskia poured coffee and got up to take the rolls from the oven.

'Pax?' she said lightly as she set them on the table.

Luke eyed her expressionlessly. 'I don't know. You tell me.'

She gave him a reluctant, apologetic smile. 'I'm not at my best right now.'

'And even at your best you're not over-affectionate where I'm concerned.' He took a roll and buttered it. 'I've often wondered why, exactly, Saskia. Is there something about my person that offends you?'

'No, of course not. It's just—' She shrugged. 'I'm off men at the moment.'

'That explains this particular moment, maybe, but you've been hostile towards me for the best part of ten years.' Luke stirred his coffee slowly, staring down into the cup. 'I always assumed it was because Marina and I hit it off so well from the first.'

'Good heavens, no,' Saskia said in genuine surprise. 'I was pleased for Mother because you obviously liked her so much. She was very nervous about you before she met you.'

Luke's eyebrows shot up. 'Was she really? I never knew that.' His eyes narrowed. 'Was *that* the problem, then? Because I made her nervous?'

Saskia sighed. 'No. I told you why before. I resented you, Lucius Armytage, because I was such an ugly duckling.'

He let out a crack of laughter. 'But that wasn't my fault, Sassy.'

'Of course it wasn't—but I still hated you.'

'Do you hate me still?' he asked, surprising her.

'No.' She smiled a little. 'At least, not so much.'

'Good.' He leaned back in his chair, scrutinising her lazily. 'And you must know, if only from the odd look in the mirror, that Saskia grown up is no ugly duckling. Though,' he added warily, 'I'm not sure about the hair.'

'You don't like my gold threads?'

'I meant the cut. I preferred that long mane of yours, Sassy.'

'It'll grow,' she said prosaically. 'Though I hope it doesn't quite yet. This particular visit to the hairdresser cost an arm and a leg, not to mention ages on a waiting list for the man who actually cut my hair.'

Luke raised an eyebrow. 'Was this for some special occasion?'

'Of course—in honour of moving in with Francis Lawford.' Saskia refilled their cups, avoiding Luke's eyes.

'So what happened?'

'I changed my mind.'

There was silence for a moment while he waited for her to say more. When she didn't Luke finished his coffee and got up. 'I must go.'

Saskia had also changed her mind about wanting to go with him. But Luke didn't ask again. He collected his jacket and she went outside with him, unsurprised when she saw the shield-shaped radiator and distinctive crimson of an Alfa-Romeo roadster. Luke, even when hiring cars, veered towards the aesthetically pleasing.

'Very nice,' she said admiringly, and gave him a head-to-toe look. 'All in keeping with your restrained elegance, stepbrother.'

'You know the motto in Italy,' he said, shrugging. 'Look your best at all times and at all costs. Image is important in this neck of the woods.' He got in the car and looked up at her.

'So, apart from a hike to the village, what are you going to do today?'

'As little as possible.' She hesitated. 'Will you be back for dinner?'

For a moment she was sure Luke meant to say no, but he nodded slowly. 'Don't go to any trouble. Something cold will be fine.'

Saskia watched the red car wind its way down the serpentine bends of the track which led from the Villa Rosa to the main road. After it had accelerated out of her view she stayed where she was for some time, her eyes on the undulating landscape with its colours of umber and ochre punctuated at intervals by dark fingers of cypress pointing up into the cobalt sky. These surroundings were no help in the present circumstances, she thought morosely. The beauty of it all was meant to be shared with a lover, not help one forget him.

She sighed impatiently and went back into the house to clear away the breakfast things, her mouth twisting a little at the hint of domesticity. Then as she was putting the dishes away she heard a car, and her eyes lit up. Luke was coming back. He must have forgotten something. And this time she would swallow her pride and ask to go with him.

But when Saskia hurried outside she found an elderly green Fiat instead of the smart Alfa-

Romeo, and she masked her disappointment with a welcoming smile for Serafina Marenghi—the plump, bustling woman employed to look after the villa.

Teenaged Carlo, who smiled shyly from behind the wheel, was taking his mother shopping, and Serafina would be happy to make any purchases required. A list was made, a bundle of lire handed over, and Saskia advised to make the most of the sunshine—since, warned Serafina, glancing skywards, it would not last much longer. Cold weather was on its way.

Left with nothing to do, and all day to do it in, Saskia took Serafina's advice. She changed her jeans and sweatshirt for a brief two-piece swimsuit, anointed herself with suncream, collected a novel and pulled one of the steamer chairs out into the sun. If nothing else she could at least augment her tan.

But the day passed very slowly. Odd, she thought, that yesterday had been spent in exactly the same way, but surely the minutes hadn't crawled by like this. A little after midday she heard the Fiat chugging its way up to the house again, and pulled on her sweatshirt and jeans to take the groceries from Carlo, who shyly handed over a paper-wrapped bundle of herbs from his mother's garden.

Saskia thanked him warmly, insisted he keep the change he proffered, and went inside with her haul. Serafina had kept to the list and added a few ideas of her own, as requested, so that the tall refrigerator now housed a salami, wafer-thin ham, slices of roast turkey breast, sausages flavoured with fennel, some buffalo mozzarella and a hunk of Parmesan. There were also several loaves of bread, some fresh rolls, a huge bag of tomatoes, some spinach, a melon, a few figs, and a dozen eggs supplied by Serafina from her own hens.

After putting away the surplus bread in the freezer, Saskia washed the spinach and steamed it lightly while she mixed eggs into extra-fine flour to make the pasta for the ravioli she intended giving Luke as a first course. Tonight, she vowed as she worked, she would be as pleasant and friendly a sister as any man could wish for. And for once it was good to have time for the kind of cooking learnt from her mother.

Marina had been born to an Italian mother and English father. Her brief marriage to a young pilot in the Royal Air Force had ended when he'd crashed during a training flight, leaving Marina widowed and six months pregnant at the age of twenty.

When the first wild agonies of grief were over Marina concentrated on making a future for herself and her child with the modest sum of money Richard Ford had left her, and set herself up in a shop which sold elegant, well-designed clothes at affordable prices. The premises she found had a small upstairs flat, and, with her mother's help with the baby, the business acumen of her accountant father and her own flair for fashion, the dress shop with the simple name 'Marina' eventually became a success.

By the time Saskia was in her teens her grandparents had sold their house in England and retired to the Villa Rosa, which her grandfather John Harding had bought for his Anna

Maria so that she could live out her remaining days in the sun of her native Tuscany.

It was around this time that Marina was asked to an Oxford dinner party where Samuel Armytage was a fellow guest. They were married a year later. Several years afterwards, to their combined shock and joy, Marina gave birth to twin boys, Jonathan and Matthew, who, unlike Luke, were the spitting image of their father.

Saskia rolled her pasta dough thinly, then pressed a rectangle of it over the *raviolatrice*, a tray with square, jagged-edged moulds which made light work of creating ravioli. Luke, she thought as she filled the hollows with spinach and ricotta cheese, followed his mother for looks, while she, according to her mother, was very much like the father she'd never known. But by complete coincidence physically Luke could well have been her brother. They were both tall, with long, narrow faces, tawny brown hair and green eyes. But her own were an opalescent almost-green, whereas Luke's were darker, the colour of moss. The resemblance, which amused Marina and Sam, had always been a source of irritation for Saskia. But if Luke harboured any views on the subject he kept them to himself.

When the ravioli were stowed away in the refrigerator, ready to cook, Saskia returned to the sun with a book and lay there until late afternoon, when a sudden drop in temperature sent her indoors for a bath—this time with the bolt firmly home on the door. By the time six o'clock was pealing in some bell-tower in the distance Saskia was dressed in white Levi's and a jade cotton shirt, her face burnished by her protracted session in the sun.

When the Alfa-Romeo came to a halt alongside the house half an hour later, Saskia was sitting amongst the pots of geraniums under the pergola. She looked up with a smile as Luke joined her.

'Hi. You look hot. Had a busy day?'

'Very. But productive. Good evening, Saskia.' He looked at her with envy, the lopsided smile lifting one corner of his mouth. 'I'm weary, travel-stained, and in much need of a shower. No need, I see, to ask how you are. You glow.'

'I've spent most of the day in the sun.'

'How was your walk to the village?'

'It didn't happen. Serafina and son went off in the car with my shopping list and saved me a trip.' She stretched a little. 'So I've done nothing all day.'

Luke sighed theatrically. 'While I've spent my time chasing round a large part of Tuscany winkling out unusual top quality beverages I can sell at reasonable prices and still make a profit.'

She grinned up at him. 'But you succeeded. You've got that satisfied look about you—the hunter home from the hill with the best catch.'

'I acquired some pretty impressive merchandise today. One so-called table wine is a real world-beater. I've got several customers waiting for it—' He stopped, laughing. 'Sorry. My hobby-horse tends to run away with me. By the way,' he added, making for the door, 'if you don't feel like cooking we can always eat out somewhere. There's a *trattoria* the other side of—'

'Certainly not,' said Saskia indignantly. 'I've been slaving away most of the day over our meal, I'd have you know.'

'I thought you said you'd been out in the sun.'

'Not *all* day,' she said demurely.

Luke leaned against one of the arches. 'So what should I be opening in the way of wine?'

'I've been reading your book on the subject,' she said smugly. 'I had a rummage down in the cellar, and some of your Dolcetto from Piedmont would be just the ticket. So I brought a bottle up. I'll open it while you're in the bath.'

'What are we having?'

'Wait and see!'

Luke gave her an amused, considering look, then excused himself and went off whistling into the house. When he returned, half an hour later, in khaki trousers and another of his thin white shirts, Saskia was sitting at the table on the terrace with an opened bottle and two glasses on the table beside her.

'I could get used to this very easily,' he remarked, and poured wine into the glasses before letting himself down beside her with a sigh. 'An evening with stars and a rising moon, with just that hint of cold to warn us to enjoy it while we may—and a beautiful woman for company. One, moreover, who is also providing dinner. I usually eat out when I'm here on my own.'

'I suppose you know a lot of people in the area.' She revolved the wine in her glass and sniffed deeply before tasting it, secretly much gratified by the compliment.

'I do. What do you think of the wine?'

'Lovely. Soft and very fruity.'

'And fairly alcoholic,' he warned.

'Don't worry. I never drink more than two glasses of anything.' Her smile was sardonic. 'Even after my experience with Francis I consoled myself with chocolate, not alcohol.'

Luke was silent for a while. 'As must be perfectly obvious, Saskia, I burn with curiosity on this particular subject. And not just because I brought you and Lawford together, either.'

'All right,' said Saskia briskly. 'After dinner I'll tell you my story if you tell me yours.'

Luke turned his head to look at her in the dusk. 'What story?'

'You and Zoë. I thought you two were headed for the altar.' She smiled at his raised eyebrows. 'She's the only one you ever brought to Christmas in Oxford. Mother was planning her wedding outfit.'

'It's a very short story,' he said dismissively. 'Not even very interesting. But, if you want to hear it, why not? Though you've never shown much interest in my private life before.'

'Nor you in mine,' she retorted, then bit her lip. Be nice, she told herself.

'Then perhaps it's time we started. Who knows?' he said lightly. 'We might be able to steer each other away from future trouble.'

Later, in the kitchen, Luke sat at the table Saskia had laid ready for dinner, watching as she slid the ravioli into boiling water and set a small pan of butter to heat.

'You can cut some bread if you like,' she remarked, while she stood, eyes glued to her watch. 'I need to time these exactly.'

'I never realised you were so skilled in the kitchen,' said Luke, slicing the loaf thickly.

'I loved helping Mother as soon as I was big enough to stand up without falling over.' Saskia smiled at him over her shoulder. 'Nonna—my grandmother—too. I had some steps I used to drag round the kitchen so I could reach the table. They both used to let me play with the left-over pasta dough, and my grandfather would eat the horrible little grey bits when it was cooked. It was a very useful skill later, when Mother was delayed in the shop in my schooldays. I often started the dinner once my homework was done. Especially when my grandparents came here to live at Villa Rosa.'

'It's a pity your grandmother didn't have longer to enjoy it,' said Luke quietly.

Saskia nodded, threw a handful of sage leaves into the butter, then drained the ravioli in a colander in the sink. 'But she loved it while she was alive. Then Grandad came home to England to live with his sister, and made this place over to Mother.'

'How is he?'

'Fine. He enjoys a game of golf still, and likes pottering about in Aunt Cora's garden, and they belong to a bridge club. And quarrel a lot—and enjoy it.' Saskia set two plates on the table, then the ravioli garnished with the butter sauce. 'Right. Let's eat. I thought something filling would go down well for the first course.'

Luke needed no second bidding. He ate in silent concentration for a while, then looked at her with deep respect. 'This is wonderful. What's in the sauce?'

'Nothing much. Butter, sage and so on. Serafina sent me some fresh herbs from her garden. But the next course, I warn you, is cold. I took you at your word.' Saskia took their plates, then brought out a platter of thinly sliced turkey, ham and salami, along with a salad of ripe red tomatoes and mozzarella cheese dressed with the local olive oil and Serafina's basil.

Luke professed himself just as happy with the second course as the first, and chatted easily during the meal about his recent visit to Bordeaux at harvest time, followed by his trip to the Rassegna del Chianti Classico—the biggest celebration of local wines in Tuscany. Before that, he told her, there had been a visit to New Zealand in the spring, and he went on to describe the prodigious tasting sessions he'd enjoyed at the various wineries there. Saskia

listened enviously—something he remarked on
after a while.

'You're an amazingly good audience,
Saskia.' He smiled. 'You and I have never
spent very long in conversation together before. Without Marina and Dad and the twins,
I mean.'

'No.' She returned the smile ruefully. 'But
I'm consumed with envy. I never realised what
an interesting life you lead. A lot more interesting than mine.'

'Then make a change.'

'I may, at that. I'll start looking when I get
back.'

They finished the meal with figs and cheese,
then cleared away together. When the big, uncluttered kitchen was tidy, Saskia made coffee
and they took it outside to drink on the terrace.
The moon was high in the sky now, but the
air was chilly, and Saskia went to her room for
a sweater before joining Luke, who was leaning in one of the archways, his eyes on the
scene before him. Up here on the hill they
could have been suspended in moonlit space.

The village below was hidden in a veil of mist which warned that summer was almost over.

'Other-worldly, isn't it?' she said softly as she stood beside him, looking up into his absorbed face. 'What are you thinking?'

'That I smell change in the air.'

Saskia nodded. 'Serafina says the cold weather's about to arrive.'

'Does she, now? That settles it. Excuse me a minute, Sassy. I have to ring someone.'

'Right.' She sat down and poured herself a coffee, while Luke went off to get his cellphone. He left his bedroom door open, and she could hear him talking to someone, the words indistinguishable but the urgency unmistakable. Then after a few minutes' conversation he laughed uproariously, and she relaxed. Nothing, it seemed, was wrong. Whoever he was talking to.

When Luke rejoined her, also wearing a sweater, he let himself down onto the wicker sofa beside her and accepted a cup of coffee with thanks. 'That's a relief. I was talking to Tom Harley, Joe's nephew.'

'In California?' she said in surprise.

'No. Right here in Tuscany. Tom's one of these flying wine makers, who alternates his trade between California and Italy. He always comes over here at this time of year for the grape harvest, but sometimes he chances his arm by leaving it too long, to make ultimate use of the sun. A few seasons ago he misjudged it badly, and lost all his grapes to unforecast bad weather. This year all is safely gathered in already, much to his wife's relief.' Luke chuckled. 'I gather he was not easy to live with for months after the disaster.'

'I can well imagine it!'

'This time he's jubilant, certain it's going to be a fabulous year. And,' Luke added, grinning, 'he's throwing a party at his place on Saturday. We're invited.'

'Really? But he doesn't know me.'

'I told him my little sister was staying here with me, so he insists I take you along.'

'Little *sister*!' snorted Saskia.

'Tom told me to emphasise that he and Lauren would be thrilled to meet you.'

'That's very nice of them,' she said, mollified. 'What sort of party?'

'Local gentry, fellow wine makers, expats of various nationality, that kind of thing.'

'Smart?'

'Probably.'

'Then I can't go. The dress I wore last night is as smart as my wardrobe here gets.'

'Then wear that.'

'No way.'

There was silence for a moment. 'I'd like you to come,' said Luke without emphasis.

'I'd like to go, too,' she admitted. 'But, trivial though it may sound, not in a dress I bought in a high street chain store. We're in Italy, remember?'

'Then let's nip into Florence tomorrow—plenty of frocks there.'

'You mean like Versace, Armani and so on?' Saskia chuckled. 'Sorry. The budget won't run to that.'

'I'll treat you to a dress. Call it your Christmas present, if you like.'

'I couldn't let you do that—'

'Why not? I *am* a relative—connection—whatever. If some other guy buys you a dress, Sassy, ten to one he means to be on hand when you take it off. But I'm your stepbrother, so there's no ulterior motive involved other than wanting you to have a good time.'

Saskia turned her eyes on him doubtfully. 'I suppose I could always pay you back later, when I get home.'

'Do I detect a hint of surrender?' he said in triumph.

She chuckled involuntarily. 'More than a hint. I give in. What woman would turn down the offer of shopping in Florence?'

He laughed, and touched her fingers lightly. 'Your tiny hand is frozen, Miss Ford. Would you like to go inside? I could light a fire.'

'No fear. This moonlight's too beautiful to waste. Besides—' she turned to look at him '—you promised to tell me about Zoë.'

# CHAPTER THREE

LUKE shrugged. 'There's no great tale of tragedy to relate. Zoë and I parted over a very basic difference of opinion. You've heard I bought a house?'

'Of course. Marina said it's charming; Sam said it needed a lot of work.'

'They're both right. Zoë took one look at it and thought I was barking mad.'

'Why?'

'It's about two hundred years old, and the minute I set eyes on it I had to have it. At time of purchase the kitchen and bathrooms had been renovated, but otherwise it needed a lot of loving care. Not Zoë's cup of tea.' Luke paused, his eyes on the view. 'She wanted a modern flat with a view of the Thames. Not my scene at all. Neither of us would budge an inch. So in the end we called it a day.'

'Were you thinking of getting married?' asked Saskia curiously.

'If we had been I assume one of us would have given in,' he said elliptically. 'The important thing would have been the fact of being together, not the location. But I made the fatal mistake of saying what fun we'd have, doing the place up bit by bit.'

Saskia tried to keep a straight face as she pictured Zoë helping Luke in overalls with a paintbrush. Zoë worked for a fashion magazine and wore elegant little suits with minuscule skirts, never a silver-blonde hair out of place.

'I told you it was boring,' he reminded her, and tapped her hand. 'Right. Your turn. What happened with Lawford?'

Saskia was quiet for a moment, reliving the day, just a week before, when her life had taken a new turn. She deliberately called up the scene, testing it as a tongue probes an aching tooth.

'I just took two suitcases to start with, and Mother drove me to the station,' she said calmly. 'It felt so—so momentous, as though one half of my life was behind me and I was setting out on a new, glamorous phase, completely different from what had gone before.

I'd sublet my flat in Chiswick, had a couple of days at home in Oxford, and suddenly I got impatient, decided to surprise Francis by starting this new life of mine a day earlier than planned.'

She had gone up in the lift in the smart building where Francis lived, clutching her suitcases and a bag of extravagant titbits collected from the nearby delicatessen. His key, handed to her over a romantic dinner days before, had been clutched in her hand like a talisman. Fizzing with anticipation, she'd let herself into the quiet, tidy flat, put down her suitcases and taken the bag of groceries into the immaculate kitchen.

'I was so thrilled with the idea of a daily cleaner,' she said derisively. 'No more chores for me after a hectic day at the bank. Sometimes since,' she said honestly, 'I've wondered if Francis's domestic arrangements weren't a major part of the attraction of moving in with him.'

'So what happened?'

'The flat was very quiet. Where I live it's a pretty busy area, with traffic noise and so on.

But Francis's place seemed insulated from all that. Zoë would love it—a doorman, views of the river from vast windows, modern furniture and rag-rolled walls. A lot different from my homely little attic.'

She had taken her cases along the narrow hall and opened the door to the master bedroom, then stopped dead, her feet rooted to the floor. The curtains were drawn, but the light filtering through them was quite sufficient to see the two people in the bed. Deeply asleep, they were clutched close in each other's arms in a tangle of naked limbs, the woman's long blonde mane mingled with the man's sweat-darkened hair, their bodies only partially covered by a rumpled sheet. A quilt and a couple of pillows were in a heap on the floor, and discarded clothes led in an explicit trail to the bed.

'Have you ever had the kind of dream,' asked Saskia conversationally, 'where however much you want to run you can't move?'

'Yes,' said Luke, looking grim.

'I don't suppose it was more than a second or two, but at last I managed to back out without waking them. I tiptoed back along the hall with my suitcases, collected my pathetic little bag of goodies and got myself out of there as fast as I could.' She smiled bitterly. 'The doorman looked rather surprised as I shot past him, but I didn't slow down until I found a taxi, and made for Paddington Station and a train back to Oxford.'

'Did you know the woman?' asked Luke, after a pause.

'Oh, yes. It was his ex-wife.' Saskia thrust her hair back with an irritable gesture. 'Not quite as ''ex'' as I thought, unfortunately. I knew he still saw Amanda from time to time. On business, he told me—things to sign, and all that. But that day it was flagrantly obvious their dealings were pleasure, not business.' She let out a deep breath. 'You know what really got to me, Luke?'

'Tell me.'

'The flat was so immaculate, so tidy. Not a newspaper or a dirty coffee cup or a used wineglass. Nothing. Yet the bedroom looked as though a bomb had hit it.' She breathed in deeply. 'The contrast was horribly vivid.

They'd obviously rushed straight from the front door to the bedroom, too intent on having sex to stop for anything other than to draw the curtains.'

'I think I'll see to him whether you want me to or not,' said Luke harshly. 'What the hell was the idiot up to? Did he think he could have you and still indulge in the odd spot of auld lang syne with the ex-wife whenever the fancy took him?'

'To be fair, the fancy obviously took them both simultaneously. I could tell from the way the clothes were discarded—' Saskia swallowed hard, suddenly sorry she'd eaten so much at dinner.

Luke reached out and grasped her hand tightly in silent comfort.

She let out a deep breath. 'What a fool I was. I really thought he cared for me. It was a big step on my part, actually moving in with Francis. But I think he's still in love with Amanda. Otherwise…'

'Otherwise?'

Saskia's face flushed with heat in the darkness. 'Well—people usually separate after making love. Disentangle themselves and so on.'

'Not necessarily.'

She shrugged. 'Anyway, even fast asleep Francis was still holding Amanda tightly, and she him. As though they couldn't bear to let go of each other. It was *that* I couldn't get out of my mind.'

'Are you still in love with him?' asked Luke neutrally.

She shook her head. 'No. Which is mortifying, in a way. I must be a very shallow sort of female. Or a very mistaken one. Whatever feelings I had for Francis didn't survive that Friday afternoon in Romney Court. It's odd. If I had seen them lunching somewhere, or even if Francis had come to me and told me what had happened—that for some reason his wife had needed comforting and one thing led to another, and so on, and it would never happen again—I would probably have been able to handle it. Because I hadn't seen for myself.' She shivered. 'But I can't forget the scene I walked in on. I'd never thought what *"in flagrante"* meant before, but that day it was brought home to me with a vengeance. I'm just grateful I didn't arrive any earlier.'

'Amen to that,' Luke said dryly, and got up. 'Come on, Sassy, let's go inside. It's cold out here.'

Saskia shivered slightly as she got to her feet. 'A good thing your Tom Harley picked his grapes, then.'

'A very good thing.' Luke followed her along the hall with the tray, his eyes searching her face when they reached the brightly lit kitchen. 'No tears?'

She shook her head, smiling. 'No. I'm not much one for tears, Luke. When I ran away from Francis that day I was swearing like a trooper, not crying.'

'How did Marina react when you turned up in Oxford again?'

'When I gave her an edited version of the scene in Francis's bedroom she lost her temper in true Latin style, and wanted to storm up to London and inflict physical injury on him. My mother's Italian half tends to dominate under certain circumstances.'

Luke grinned. 'I know.'

'But that was just gut reaction.' Saskia shrugged. 'When she calmed down she became intensely practical, as always, and suggested I come here to lick my wounds, since I'd already arranged to be away from my job for a fortnight. Francis was going to take time off, too, you see, so we could enjoy playing house for a while.' She breathed in deeply. 'Sam was wonderful. He arranged a plane flight, bless him, and drove me to the airport. So here I am. Mending my broken heart at the Villa Rosa.'

'Is it really broken?'

'No.' She managed a creditable little laugh. 'Dented a bit, maybe, but not broken. And I've learned a very valuable lesson—no more falling in love.'

Luke smiled a little. 'Not until the next time, anyway.'

'Something like that.'

'Right then, Saskia,' he said briskly. 'No more moping alone here. Come with me tomorrow.'

'Where?'

'I'll drive you to San Gimignano, then you can browse round the town while I chase up some of the local wine. It shouldn't take long. I'll buy you lunch afterwards.'

Saskia smiled. 'Sounds good. Thanks; I'd like that.'

Luke raised an eyebrow, as though he'd expected opposition. 'Good. I'll say goodnight, then, Sassy.' He paused, looking down at her steadily. 'I'm glad you told me.'

'So am I.' She hesitated. 'And I'm sorry it didn't work out with Zoë.'

'Thank you. Though I feel it only fair to mention that my heart isn't broken either.'

'I didn't think it was.' She grinned. 'It's you who does the heartbreaking, from all I hear.'

'Certainly not,' he said virtuously. 'I'm really a very nice, kind sort of chap.'

'Oh, yeah?' Laughing, Saskia went off to bed, feeling a great deal better than at any time since her flight from Romney Court.

Next morning Saskia woke early, with a feeling of anticipation she realised came from the proposed outing with Luke. Her mother would be surprised, she thought, smiling as she dressed. Marina was always defending Luke to her daughter, never able to understand why Saskia wasn't as charmed by him as she was.

'You were up early,' said Luke accusingly as he came into the kitchen later. 'I crept around like a mouse not to disturb you, and here you are, up with the lark.'

'If this sunshine's likely to end soon I want to make the most of it. Want some tea? Proper British tea? I brought it with me.'

'Right, then,' said Luke, after breakfast. 'Let's be on our way.'

They were both dressed in jeans and white shirts, Saskia with a pale green sweater knotted round her shoulders, Luke carrying a jacket over his arm.

'Will I do?' she asked mockingly. 'Do I come up to scratch?'

'You certainly do.' He held the car door for her, his eyes making a leisurely survey from her expensive haircut to her gleaming leather shoes. 'I take it you've decided to stop wasting time on regrets over Lawford?'

'Of course I have,' she said irritably, and slid into the passenger seat of the Alfa-Romeo. 'Let's not mention him again. I want to enjoy the day.'

'Amen to that.' Luke drove down the hairpin bends from the house to the main road, his skill at the wheel coming as no surprise to Saskia.

'Other than in a taxi, I've never been in a car with you before,' she remarked as he turned on to the road which would take them to the hilltop town of San Gimignano.

'Not surprising. At times in the past I had the impression you hated being in the same room, let alone the same car.'

'I've grown up a bit now. And if it's any consolation I think you drive very well. But then,' she added tartly, 'one of the reasons I used to resent you was the fact that you do *everything* well.'

Luke laughed. 'The secret of my success is simple—I make it a rule only to do things well within my capacity. I knew I could never be an academic, like Dad, but I had a feeling for wine from my first trip to the Napa Valley. So,

I'm a success at what I do because it interests me, I work damned hard, and I've got a reasonable head for business.'

'And a knack of knowing what people want so you can supply it.'

'True.' He gave her a sidelong glance. 'Do you realise, Saskia Ford, that you said something very important just now?'

'Did I? What, exactly?'

'You said you *used* to resent me.'

Saskia said nothing for a moment, her eyes on the ageless beauty of the scenery unfolding before her. 'So I did,' she said slowly. 'Since you arrived at the Villa Rosa you've been very kind. Different, somehow. Especially last night. I feel better since I got all that stuff off my chest.'

'Good.' He glanced at her again. 'Do you want me to put the hood up? Your haircut is suffering a bit.'

'No fear!' She laughed, thrusting her hands through her streaming hair. 'All my cobwebs are blowing away.'

Luke drove her to one of the car parks below the town, and Saskia went off on foot to explore, promising to meet him in the Piazza della Cisterna at midday.

San Gimignano, the 'city of beautiful towers', had retained only fourteen of the original seventy-six, but otherwise looked much the same in the morning sunshine as it had done since the thirteenth century. Saskia's previous visit here had been a brief one with her grandparents several years before, and she was glad to find the hilltop town unchanged. The two main streets still retained their medieval feel, with shops displaying boars' heads and the local wine, others selling hand-woven fabrics and locally made ceramics. There were galleries selling jewellery and paintings, and here and there was an artist seated at an easel, painting watercolour views of the town.

She strolled through the streets, stopping to browse in the tempting shops every so often, wondering if Luke would fancy a visit to the *duomo* after lunch. There was a wealth of frescoed paintings to be seen in there, she knew, but exploration was better done in company in the awe-inspiring cathedrals of Italy.

Saskia lingered to watch one of the artists at work, and bought a watercolour for her mother and Sam. She chose a view of the many-towered skyline of San Gimignano, with a cleverly executed backdrop of the country-side beyond, exchanged a few words with the artist, then wandered on again and bought wild boar pâté in a dark cavern of a shop, postcards for the twins in another.

The entire town was a living museum, and it was pleasure enough just to wander through the streets in the cool sunshine, looking at the beauty of the ancient buildings, none of which dated from later than the fourteenth century.

When she reached the Piazza della Cisterna, Saskia ordered mineral water at one of the res-taurants, and sat down to write her postcards at a table outside so she could keep an eye out for Luke. She scribbled away busily, and prompt to the minute, as midday began to toll, a shadow fell across her table, and she looked up to see him smiling down at her.

'Hello, Sassy. Have you been waiting long?'

'I was early, and who could mind hanging about in a place like this?'

'What have you been doing?'

'Just browsing in the shops, mainly. But I got this for Mother and Sam from the artist working near the *duomo*.' She took out the watercolour to show him. 'And I bought a present for you, too.'

Luke eyed her for a moment, surprised. 'A present?' he said guardedly.

Saskia chuckled, and handed him the pâté. 'I hope you like it.'

His lips twitched as he thanked her gravely. 'My favourite,' he assured her. 'Come on, I'm hungry. A gentle little stroll will take us to a place where we can eat under a pergola of vines.'

Because it was early they were given the best table in the restaurant, with a panoramic view of central Tuscany to add to the pleasure of the food.

'But no wine at this time of day for me,' said Saskia as she studied the menu.

'We shall both keep to virtuous mineral water,' he agreed. 'The driver will content himself with thoughts of wild boar pâté for supper.'

'You don't *have* to eat it!' she assured him, chuckling. 'I won't be offended if you loathe it.'

Luke shook his head in wonder. 'I can't quite believe this new, mellow you, Saskia. I keep expecting that sharp tongue of yours to lash out at any minute.' He grinned. 'It adds a certain piquancy to proceedings.'

She grinned back, waggling the tip of her tongue at him outrageously.

'Don't do that,' he said abruptly.

'Sorry,' she said, startled. 'I didn't mean—'

'I know. And this is me, so no problem. But don't try it with other men.'

'Too rude?'

He shook his head. 'Too provocative. Now, what do you fancy to eat? This place is known for its truffles and mushrooms.'

'Sounds good. I rarely eat meat in Italy; they have so many fabulous dishes with vegetables,' said Saskia rapidly, feeling oddly disorientated by Luke's rebuke. 'Tagliolini with *tartuffi* and *porcini*, then.'

Luke chose the same, then sat back in his chair, looking at Saskia's averted face as she studied the breathtaking view. 'So what else did you buy?' he asked, deliberately conversational.

'Just postcards.' She turned with a smile, determined to preserve this new, precarious amity with Luke. 'Have you somewhere else to go today?'

'No. I've sorted out my wine supplies, and that's about it for this trip. My time is at your disposal. If you want it,' he added, the lopsided smile in evidence.

'I do, actually. Will you come and look round the *duomo* with me this afternoon? I didn't fancy it on my own.' She smiled ruefully. 'I wasn't old enough to appreciate it when my grandparents brought me here. I was in rebellious teenager mode at the time.'

'I remember it well,' he said lightly. 'And as it happens I'd very much like to explore the *duomo*.' His mouth went down at the corners. 'Would you believe I've never been inside the place?'

Saskia stared at him in surprise. 'But you're always tripping back and forth to Tuscany.'

'I tend to make flying visits, purely on business, alas. I rarely have time to do the culture bit as well.' He paused as their pasta was served, then gave her a very direct look. 'Look, Sassy, I quite fancy doing some of the usual tourist things here now the summer crowds have gone. You're on your own. I've given myself a few days off. I vote we join forces.'

Saskia looked at him in surprise. 'Do you really want to do that?' She flushed. 'I mean, you're not just being kind because of Francis?'

'No,' he said with exaggerated patience, 'I am not. In fact I suggest you forget the prat ever existed. I've got the car, so we could go as far as Urbino, or there's Arezzo—and Florence, of course. We mustn't forget the dress.'

She tasted a mouthful of her pasta thoughtfully, more pleased with Luke's suggestion than she would ever have imagined possible. 'I'd like that very much,' she said at last, after the first, delicious mouthful had gone down.

'Good. That's settled,' he said briskly, and applied himself to his lunch. 'This, Miss Ford, is almost as good as the pasta you made for me.'

'Which is quite a compliment, because this is wonderful.'

Luke grinned. 'I meant it, nonetheless. Somehow I've never associated you with skill in the kitchen.'

Her eyes narrowed. 'Where did you think my skills lay, then? If any?'

'In your posh merchant bank, of course. All that high-powered finance and so on.'

Saskia looked around her at the crowded restaurant, where local inhabitants were giving serious concentration to the delights on offer. She looked out again at the view, then returned to her plate, shaking her head. 'At this moment in time the FT index, and the Nikkei and Dow Jones seem like things from another planet. The people here look as though food is a far more important factor in life than the stock-market.'

'Add wine, sex, music and football—though not necessarily in that order—and you're probably right.' Luke's eyes gleamed with laughter, reflecting the green of the overhead ceiling of vines.

Saskia chuckled. 'It's definitely time I changed my job.'

'I wish I had one to offer you, but my own personal assistant is a very efficient lady, and very knowledgeable about wines. I could hardly boot her out to indulge in nepotism and give her job to you,' said Luke with regret.

'I should think not!' Saskia eyed him challengingly. 'Is she pretty?'

'Very. So are her teenage daughters. And a large, possessive husband drops her off every morning.'

'Oh.' Saskia shrugged apologetically. 'Somehow I'd imagined you surrounded by employees like Zoë.'

'Far from it. Though I'm amazed you thought of me in any context,' he said, scouring his plate with a large hunk of bread. 'But I'll keep my ear to the ground. If I do hear of anything less frenetic in the job line, I'll let you know.'

On the point of telling him she was perfectly capable of finding her own job, Saskia held her tongue and reminded herself that it was time she stopped snapping Luke's head off at every opportunity. She was no longer fifteen years old. And Luke, for the first time in their acquaintance, was treating her like an equal, instead of an irritating younger sister.

'I'd be grateful,' she said, and sat back with a sigh. 'I'm going to have to stop eating all this pasta. I'll never get into any of my office suits at this rate. And I'll need to for a while, because I've no intention of quitting my job before I find another.'

'Very sensible.' Luke eyed her steadily. 'But you won't have any problem with that.'

'I hope not.' She shrugged. 'I've been at the bank for three years. It's a bit scary to think of putting myself in the market place again.'

'You possess experience in a very prestigious kind of job, you look good and you dress well.' He smiled. 'I imagine most employers in need of your kind of expertise would snap you up the minute they laid eyes on you.'

'That's very comforting.' She smiled cajolingly. 'Now, in spite of the calories, could I have a pudding? I haven't eaten anything sweet since I pigged out on chocolate after finding Francis in bed with his wife.' She giggled suddenly. 'How silly that sounds.'

'If you can laugh about it, you're over it,' Luke assured her, and signalled to a waiter. 'What would you like?'

After an earnest discussion with the waiter Saskia chose *panna cotta*, the universal, creamy pudding of Italy, this time served with chestnuts in a red wine sauce. 'And tonight,' she said firmly, 'I shan't have any dinner. Not that I mind rustling up something for you, though.'

'My word, Saskia,' teased Luke. 'I can hardly credit the change in you. Are you likely to revert when we get back to London? I hope not.'

'Why?'

'I prefer you this way, little sister. I begin to see why there was always a line of hopefuls beating their way to your door.' He was suddenly very serious. 'Though why you settled on Lawford rather than any of the others is a complete mystery to me.'

'It is to me now,' she said morosely. 'Why on earth I fell in love with him in particular I don't know. But I did. Which has taught me a salutary lesson—I'll never trust my emotions again.'

'Don't say that, Sassy. You're too attractive to give up on men altogether.'

'I don't intend to.' Saskia smiled at him sweetly. 'In future the man can do the falling in love. I'll just bask in the glow and keep my heart to myself.'

# CHAPTER FOUR

WHEN Saskia used Luke's phone to ring her mother next morning, Marina Armytage was aghast at the news that her stepson had arrived at the Villa Rosa.

'Oh *darling*. What a thing. I was so worried about you when you left I forgot Luke might need to stay, too. But just for once be good, Saskia,' she added with emphasis. 'Try to exist under the same roof for a night without coming to blows. Please?'

When her daughter said casually that not only had Luke already been in residence for two days, but he was staying for several more, Marina was rendered speechless.

'Are you still there, Mother?' demanded Saskia.

'Yes,' said Marina faintly. She cleared her throat. 'I suppose Luke won't be in your way much. He must be out a lot on business.'

'Actually he's not,' said Saskia, enjoying herself. 'He's finished that part of the trip. He's taking a few days' holiday. Sightseeing with me today and tomorrow. Then on Saturday we're going to a party at Tom Harley's to celebrate their grape harvest. Tom is Joe Harley's nephew.'

After several more protestations of amazement, followed by solicitous enquiries about her daughter's health, both physical and mental, Marina, who had not been involved in the fashion business for nothing, suddenly remembered that Saskia's luggage contained nothing remotely suitable for a party. 'The brown dress won't do,' she warned.

'I know.' Saskia felt a great bubble of mirth rise up inside her. 'Don't worry. Luke's promised to buy me a dress in Florence. I really must go, Mother. This is his phone.'

After saying her goodbyes to her astonished parent, and sending love to Sam and the twins, Saskia went outside on the terrace to give the phone back to Luke, and collapsed into a chair, laughing.

'What's so funny?' he demanded.

'My mother,' gurgled Saskia. 'You should have heard her! Not that you could for a while. The news that we were here at the villa together struck her dumb. Then I mentioned the party, and the joint sightseeing, and topped it off with your offer to buy me a dress. I bet she's ringing Sam at this moment, incoherent with astonishment.'

Luke leaned in one of the archways, his eyes gleaming with amusement. 'But was she pleased or otherwise?'

'Oh, pleased. Definitely.' Saskia gave him a glinting little smile. 'She's very fond of you. As you well know.'

'I do know. And I reciprocate.' He gave her a very straight look. 'At least she knows perfectly well that *I*'ll take care of you.' He glanced at his watch. 'Come on, Sassy, jump to it—time we were off. So which do you fancy? Arezzo or Urbino?'

Saskia discovered that a trip to the famously beautiful town of Urbino, in the province of the Marches, meant a drive over the Alpe della Luna. Despite the allure of a route named 'mountains of the moon', Saskia opted for

Arezzo, which was neither as far nor as demanding as the dizzying climb and descent involved in reaching the stronghold of the Duke of Urbino, who had been the patron of Piero della Francesca.

'Not,' she said, smiling, 'that I'm casting aspersions on your driving, Luke, but at this time of the year there's bound to be mist up on those mountains, even on a sunny day like this. I'm not ecstatic about hairpin bends even when they're visible.'

'Then Arezzo it is. It's a shorter journey, so we can get back fairly early and go out to dinner somewhere this evening,' said Luke.

'Could we just have a big lunch and not go out tonight?' said Saskia. 'Not that I mind if you want to, of course,' she added hastily. 'I know you've got friends here. I'll be perfectly happy on my own with a book.'

Luke eyed her challengingly. 'Would you prefer that?'

'*No!*' she said, so vehemently she flushed a little. 'Of course not. I just thought you might have had enough of my undiluted company by then, that's all.'

'The novelty hasn't worn off yet,' he said lightly.

Arezzo, on the other side of the *autostrada* from Florence and Siena, was less overrun by tourists than the more popular Tuscan attractions—and Saskia, who had never been there before, was disappointed at first glance by the modern development on the approach to the city. But once inside the walls they were transported back in time as they reached the heart of what had once been a medieval and Renaissance stronghold.

After Luke had found a parking place he considered worthy of the car, they made their way up the main shopping street, the Corso Italia, to the Piazza Grande. The main square sloped down towards them from an impressive arcaded portico, with medieval houses on one side facing the exquisite church of Santa Maria della Pieve on the other.

'The fabulous portico was designed by local hero Giorgio Vasari. His house is here somewhere, too,' said Saskia, consulting her guide book. 'Could we go to the church of San

Francesco first? Piero's most important frescos are in there—the Legend of the True Cross.'

'Lead on,' said Luke. 'I hope you've got plenty of coins.'

'Oh, of course,' said Saskia, searching in her handbag. 'We need them for the lights.'

The interior of the thirteenth-century church was dark behind the austere façade it showed to the world, and regular injections of money into the slot lighting were necessary in the chapel where Piero della Francesca had painted the frescoes just over five hundred years earlier. Dimmer and more time-ravaged than they appeared in glossy art books, with patches of bare wall in places, the frescos were nevertheless miracles to marvel at. One panel, more visible than the rest, showed the Dream of Constantine, with the emperor and his guards bathed in heavenly light.

'This,' said Luke, studying it with respect, 'is supposed to be one of the first night paintings.'

'My favourite, I think,' whispered Saskia. 'Oh, look, that's the Queen of Sheba, recognising the cross. And there she is again, shaking hands with—who?'

'Whom,' corrected Luke severely, peering at the guide book. 'Solomon—who else? Didn't they do rather more than just shake hands?'

'This,' she hissed, poking him in the ribs, 'is a church, Lucius Armytage. Which bit of fresco do you like best?'

'The battle scene,' he decided after a while. 'Renaissance warfare was a chaotic business. Not,' he added, sobering, 'that I suppose it's ever anything else. There's just more technology along with the mayhem these days.'

When their supply of coins ran out they went in search of a late lunch, which they found nearby in a basement restaurant with low, vaulted ceilings, candles on tables laid with starched white cloths, and more frescos on the walls. When Saskia found it hard to choose from the dishes on offer, the waiter suggested they both try an *assaggio*—a taste of several of the house specialities—accompanied by wine from the restaurant cellar.

The suggestion found favour with both of them, and they fell to with gusto on *panzanella*—a delicious salad with tomatoes and slices of oil-soaked break—followed by croutons of toast topped with *finocchiona*, the local Tuscan sausage. Next they ate *farro*, traditional cereal soup, and then a dish which Saskia took to be chicken with herbs and artichokes, but was actually a traditional local recipe for rabbit, the waiter informed her with a smile when he took the empty dishes away.

'Goodness,' she said, wide-eyed. 'That's a first. I've never eaten rabbit before.'

Luke chuckled. 'You seemed to enjoy it.'

'I thought it was chicken!' She blew out her cheeks. 'Whatever it was, I can't eat another thing. I'm not sure I can even move for a while.'

'Then don't.' Luke leaned back on the settle beside her, stretching out his long legs. 'Arezzo will be sleeping for a while, anyway, so let's linger over some good Italian coffee while our lunch goes down.' He yawned a little. 'I didn't realise sightseeing was so exhausting.'

Saskia chuckled. 'Are you sure you can manage Florence tomorrow?'

'Oh, yes,' he said comfortably, eyes closed. 'As long as you don't expect me to stand in line to look at paintings in the Uffizi, or David in the Accademia. You must have done all that before.'

'More than once. I used to spend part of every school holiday here with the grandparents, remember, after Mother married Sam.'

'Is that why you were rebellious? Because you were pushed from the nest, so to speak?'

'No. My friends envied my Italian holidays madly. But I was at the age when it's the done thing to be difficult, I suppose. Hopefully I've grown more amenable since.'

'Until recently I would have disagreed with that,' he said frankly, and turned half-closed eyes on her profile.

She stirred her coffee intently. 'And now?'

'At this particular moment in time, Saskia, I couldn't ask for better company. Whether this idyllic state survives the entire time we're together—or even the rest of the day—remains to be seen.'

'True.' She turned her head to smile at him. 'But I promised Mother I'd try not to come to blows with you. So you're quite safe.'

He grinned. 'Then I needn't quake in my bed at night.'

She pulled a face. 'Very definitely not. In future I'll never set foot in any bedroom other than my own, believe me.'

Luke put a hand on hers. 'Forget him, Sassy.'

'I will, soon enough.' She shrugged. 'The wound didn't go very deep. I was embarrassed and angry more than hurt. Which served me right for being in the right place at the wrong time.'

Luke was silent for a while. The last of the other diners had left, and they were alone in their vaulted alcove. 'Talking of which,' he said slowly, staring straight ahead, 'it's time *I* apologised for doing much the same when I first arrived at the villa.'

Saskia bit her lip. 'Ah. You mean our first encounter in the bathroom? I almost expired with fright on the spot.'

He let out a snort of laughter. 'I can't say fright was my own reaction. I didn't recognise you for a moment.'

'It's only months since you saw me last,' she retorted. 'I haven't changed *that* much.'

'I wasn't looking at your face, Sassy!'

The face in question went crimson, but the appearance of the waiter with another pot of coffee spared Luke assault with a heavy candlestick.

'Count yourself lucky,' Saskia muttered ominously, once they were alone. 'You nearly had a black eye to sport at the party.'

'I was merely being truthful,' he said, unrepentant. 'It was only when I was legging it back down the hall that it dawned on me who you were.'

'Who else could it have been?'

'The villa could have been let out to someone for a holiday.'

'Mother can't be bothered these days. Says it's too much trouble. Anyway,' she added, refilling their coffee cups, 'it doesn't matter. But if you had known I was in residence I imagine you'd have given the Villa Rosa a wide berth.'

'Probably,' he admitted honestly. 'But not because *I* objected to *your* company, Sassy.

You were the one who always made it clear you objected to mine.'

Saskia knew this was true. 'Silly, really,' she said, shaking her head. 'I adore the twins, of course, but now I begin to see advantages in having a *big* brother, too.'

Luke stared at the frescoed wall in silence for a while, then gave her the crooked smile which was so much part of his attraction. Something, she realised, she could now acknowledge without a trace of the resentment she'd once felt towards him.

'So is that the role you want to play at Tom's bash on Saturday? My little sister?'

'Since I am neither little, nor your actual sister, probably not.' She shrugged. 'But I don't mind if that's what you'd prefer. Would my presence as the more normal female companion restrict your activities, perhaps?'

Luke chuckled. 'It might well do. No one seeing me arrive with you would think I'd have any interest in anyone else.'

Saskia stared at him, arrested.

He returned the look very steadily, an eyebrow raised in query. 'What's the matter?'

'You sound as though you mean that.'

'I do. I'd never really thought about it before, but I assure you that the ugly duckling has turned into the best-looking swan in town.' He grinned, and Saskia returned the smile, more pleased than she cared to show.

'Thank you, kind sir. Coming from you, that's praise indeed.'

'What do you mean, coming from me?'

'Merely that all your girlfriends have been very decorative. Offhand I can't remember one who had more brains than looks.'

He shook his head at her reprovingly. 'You didn't meet them all, Saskia! Not,' he added with sudden sincerity, 'that there were ever that many. I like women. But that's as far as it goes. Cleaving unto one for life is not, at time of going to press, an idea that appeals. The thought of marriage scares the hell out of me.'

'Amen to that!' she agreed with feeling, and gave him a coaxing smile. 'Luke, would you mind if we deserted art for a while and had a look round the shops? My guide book says a lot of gold jewellery is produced round here.'

'What are we waiting for?' he said promptly, and called the waiter over.

After a pleasurable browse through tempting shops they made their way towards the *duomo* for the obligatory look at Piero's fresco of Mary Magdalene. The sun had disappeared, and without a car in sight the mist-wreathed Renaissance buildings in the piazza presented a scene which would have been much the same five hundred years earlier. Inside the cathedral, it was hard at first to find the fresco, which was sandwiched between a fourteenth-century tomb and the sacristy door. The figure of the Magdalene gazed at them from under downcast lids, a lantern in one hand, the other holding the folds of her red mantle. Saskia shivered suddenly, and Luke took her hand.

'Cold?'

'Not really. I was just wondering how many people have stood here over the centuries, gazing up at her on the wall.'

'Too many to count. Though she's smaller than I expected.' Luke looked down into

poured coffee. 'Was that another of your reasons for hating me?' he asked, and handed the cup to her once she'd propped herself up.

She sipped the coffee with relish. 'Who could hate a man who makes coffee like this?'

He bowed theatrically. 'Then my effort wasn't in vain. Don't be too long. Parking in Florence can take patience, so we'd better be off soon if we're to hunt down this dress of yours.'

Saskia buttered a roll, eyeing him doubtfully. 'Are you sure you want to do this? Most men run a mile at the thought of shopping.'

'So do I, generally.' He went to the door, and turned to look at her. 'But just this once I'll make an exception.'

'Thank you, kind sir. Thank you for breakfast, too,' she added belatedly. 'I didn't get to sleep too quickly last night, which is why I overslept.'

'Mourning for your lost love?'

'No. Congratulating myself on a lucky escape.'

Twenty minutes later Saskia joined Luke outside on the terrace, dressed in fawn linen trousers and an ivory silk shirt, a matching linen jacket over her arm.

Since Luke was wearing a jacket in much the same shade, the similarity in their looks was even more pronounced than usual.

'We look like twins,' she said, pulling a face.

'Do you mind?'

'Not really.' She smiled up at him. 'Tell me what you're wearing to this party, and I'll look for a dress to match.'

'Good idea,' he said evenly. 'Then everyone will know we belong together.'

'I wouldn't want to spoil your fun, Luke.'

'You won't,' he assured her. 'So, come on, let's get going. The shops close at one, remember, and don't open again until late afternoon.'

Once on the *autostrada* the Alfa-Romeo ate up the miles to Florence with ease, and when they reached the city Luke was lucky enough to find a space in the underground car park at the Santa Maria Novella station.

'Right then, Sassy,' he said as they emerged into the noise and bustle of Florence in the crisp, cool-edged sunshine. 'From here on we walk.'

'Not much of a hardship in Florence,' she assured him. 'Nowhere's much more than ten minutes away from anywhere else.' She grasped his arm and held up a foot. 'And, as you can see, I'm wearing smart, *flat* Italian shoes.'

'Well polished, just like mine,' said Luke with approval. 'They think a lot of their foot-wear in this part of the world.'

Saskia nodded, feeling suddenly very happy. The crowded, medieval streets of Florence were an aesthetic delight, as usual, the sun was shining and she was strolling along beside a man who was, she decided secretly, a lot more attractive than the majority of men they passed on their way to the Ponte Vecchio. On the famous thronged bridge Luke led her past the jewellers with their fabulous wares to a shop selling silk ties.

'I'll treat myself to a new one for Tom's party,' he said, pausing to look in the window. 'Which do you fancy?'

Having established that Luke's suit was a pale biscuit shade, Saskia went inside with him to inspect the enormous selection on offer, and eventually, after much conferring, they emerged with a handsome tie in woven cinnamon silk embossed with striking gilt fleurs-de-lys.

'Right. Your turn,' said Luke. 'I assume you know where to look?'

'I certainly do.' Saskia knew from past experience that the best window shopping in Italy could be done in the Via della Vigna Nuova and the Via de' Tornabuoni, where some of the most famous names in fashion had shops which glowed like jewels in the ancient buildings which formed their setting.

Saskia gazed at length at the offerings in Armani, Valentino and Gucci, the shoes in Ferragamo, but steered Luke firmly away to names less well known, where she hoped the prices might be less astronomical.

'The really pricey stuff will only be to order anyway,' he reminded her. 'So find something ready to wear that you like, and choose a style and colour you won't grow tired of too quickly.'

Saskia looked up at him in amusement. 'You're very knowledgeable on the subject, Lucius Armytage!'

He grinned. 'I came here with Marina once, when she managed to leave Dad and the boys at the villa and skive off for a morning with me. She was perfectly happy just gazing in shop windows, instead of the more cultural stuff Dad likes. Your lady mother knows a lot about clothes.'

Saskia nodded, pulling a face. 'She wasn't so surprised by our truce she forgot I'd brought nothing suitable for a party.'

Eventually Luke said firmly that window shopping was over and a stab at the real thing was necessary if they were going to find a dress before lunch. 'If not, we'll have to linger over our meal until about three-thirty when these places open their doors again.'

'By which time I would need a bigger size,' she said, laughing. 'All right. You choose, Luke. Which one shall we try first?'

After a couple of unsuccessful sorties, where they were shown once-seen, never-forgotten creations, Luke steered her towards Valentino, where Saskia found two dresses she liked so much she asked Luke to choose.

'No,' he said firmly. 'I've been caught like that before, with Zoë. If I choose one, you'll have regrets about the other one.'

'I,' said Saskia astringently, 'am not Zoë.'

'Very true. So go and try them on and see which one feels most like you.'

Much as she loved the brief little shift in the famous Valentino red, Saskia chose a flirty little slip dress in black silk chiffon with shoulder straps of gilt satin. It was knee-skimming, flattering and so dateless that with luck, Saskia told herself, she could wear it for the next ten years. And although it was expensive she could well afford to pay Luke back for it, provided she stayed on at the bank for a while before seeking pastures new.

'You didn't model it for me,' said Luke when they were outside in the midday sunshine.

Saskia had felt oddly shy about showing herself off in the dress. 'You can see it to-morrow night when I've done my hair and I'm wearing the right shoes.' She smiled at him coaxingly. 'Would you mind staying on here until the shops open again, Luke? Cinderella needs slippers. And this time—forgive the pun—she insists on footing the bill.'

'Done. Where do you want to eat lunch? Any preferences?'

'One of the outside tables at the Rivoire in the Piazza della Signoria, if possible, please. I love watching the world go by.'

Lucius Armytage was one of that breed of men for whom waiters flock and a table always becomes free—something which had, in the past, featured on the list of things that Saskia resented about him. Now, as a waiter in a white jacket led them to the best possible table for eating, viewing and protection from over-friendly pigeons, it was a feature of the Armytage charm she found very agreeable. Francis had always made a big thing of snapping fingers and demanding attention, but with Luke it was unnecessary.

'This do you?' he asked casually as he held her chair for her.

'Perfect. Now I can look at the statues of Neptune and company, do my people-watching and eat all at the same time.' Saskia looked him in the eye as he settled himself opposite her. 'Luke, thank you for my dress. I shall pay you back in London, I promise.'

'We'll see,' he said noncommittally as a waiter materialised at his elbow with bottles of mineral water. 'Now, then, Sassy, what would you like to eat?'

She opted for pasta with meat sauce, but Luke chose *Bistecca alla Fiorentina*, the wonderful local steak, seasoned with oil and herbs and grilled over an open fire. 'I'll be good and order a salad if you'll share it with me,' he offered.

In the end they shared everything, Saskia trading some of her pasta for a piece of steak, and Luke asking for an extra spoon so he could eat some of the inevitable tiramisu Saskia chose for pudding.

'I have to eat tiramisu once while I'm here,' she declared, scraping the last of it from the dish. 'And this is gorgeous—nothing like the stuff they sell in the supermarket near my flat. The tomatoes were so wonderful too. Are they grown with special fertiliser here, or something?'

'Yes,' said Luke, deadpan. 'It's called sunshine.'

She giggled, then bit her lip, eyeing her empty wine glass. 'Maybe that second glass was a mistake. I'm getting all girly.'

'Someone had to drink it. The driver was forced to keep to one.'

'Poor you.' Saskia leaned back in her chair with a sigh of contentment, gazing at the colourful passing show with its backdrop of medieval buildings. 'On a day like this I'm always convinced I could live here for ever. Then I think of it sizzling in August and being bitterly cold in winter, and I fly back reluctantly to my London nest.'

'You must come and see mine. The new house, I mean. Not,' he added wryly, 'that there's much new about it for the time being. Are you any good at interior decorating?'

'I don't know. I've never tried. Mine's a furnished flat. Why?' She looked at him enquiringly. 'Would you like some help?'

'Would you give it?'

'Yes. If you'd like me to.' She frowned. 'That's a very funny look in your eyes, Luke.'

'I just find it hard to believe, now and then, that this is the same Saskia Ford who once couldn't manage a civil word for me,' he said bluntly.

'People change,' she said evasively. 'And we've never really spent any time together before.'

'True. Maybe if we had you might have thawed sooner.'

'Did it bother you?' she asked curiously. 'That I was so unfriendly, I mean?'

Luke gave her a very straight look. 'To be honest, not very much, Saskia. I can't say I was cut to the quick because the renowned Armytage charm failed to work on a teenaged stepsister.'

'It's a long time since I was a teenager,' she murmured, looking away across the thronged piazza.

'Ten years since we met, I know. But keeping out of your way became a habit early on, just to make things easier for our respective parents.' He reached across and touched her hand. 'So in a way I'm rather grateful for Lawford's fall from grace. It's given us a chance to find out we don't dislike each other very much after all.'

Saskia smiled at him mischievously. 'Early days, yet, Armytage.'

'I think we'll manage to keep to the cease-fire.' He looked up, and, as always, a waiter appeared instantly to take Luke's order for coffee.

When they decided that comfortable though they were they could linger no longer, they went off in search of shoes. Luke fancied some wildly impractical gilt sandals with fragile straps and spike heels, but Saskia shook her head, laughing, and chose elegantly cut black suede pumps with heels which would let her dance all night if necessary.

'Will there be dancing?' she asked afterwards.

'No idea. Probably. Tom and Lauren give great parties.'

'You've been to one before?'

'I certainly have.'

Saskia stopped suddenly, to the danger of several passers-by. 'Luke—I won't be over-dressed, will I?'

'No.' He smiled down at her, and took her arm. 'Besides, even if the other women turn up in designer jeans, you just make 'em feel they're the ones out of step.'

'I'm supposed to be reassured?' she retorted, laughing.

'Of course you are. Let's buy some food to take home. Fancy a spit-roasted chicken?'

When they got back to the villa they found it gleaming and immaculate from Serafina's attentions. After the food was put away and the new dress hung with reverence in Saskia's wardrobe, she went to the kitchen to make tea, and took it out on the terrace where Luke was reading *The Times* newspaper he'd bought in Florence.

'I'm tired,' she said, subsiding on the sofa. 'Enjoying oneself is quite exhausting.'

'So you did enjoy today, then,' he said, the smile lifting one side of his mouth.

'A day in Florence, new dress and shoes, a delicious lunch in the open air—and good company,' she added deliberately, pouring tea. 'How could I not enjoy it?'

'Are you always so appreciative when someone buys you a dress?' he enquired, stretching out a hand for his cup.

'Oh, yes. Ask my mother. She's the only other person who ever has,' she said tartly.

'Put your claws in, Sassy,' he said, unmoved.

She sniffed. 'Did you buy clothes for Zoë?'

'Oddly enough, no. I've never bought a dress for anyone before. You're the first.'

'And the last, too, I imagine, at prices like that.' She looked at him in sudden alarm. 'What if someone drops cigarette ash on me, or spills wine?'

'Then they do, you muggins. It's only a dress.'

'It's such a beautiful dress, though,' she said, her eyes gleaming. 'I feel quite wonderful in it.'

'I look forward to seeing you in it.' Luke glanced at the rapidly darkening sky. 'What do you want to do tonight? Fancy trying the *trattoria* in the village?'

Saskia shook her head. 'I'm not stirring another step. And tonight, Lucius Armytage, you can eat the chicken you bought, and I shall dine very frugally indeed. If I go on eating like this I shan't be able to zip the dress up, and that would be a tragedy.'

Luke stretched luxuriously. 'I can't say I'm sorry. A peaceful evening is probably a good idea to get in trim for tomorrow night.' He frowned suddenly. 'You obviously haven't hired a car, Saskia, so how did you intend getting around on your own? Surely you weren't intending to hole up here for your entire stay?'

'Of course not. I would have asked Serafina's Carlo to give me a lift to the station and caught a train, used taxis and so on. But I hadn't felt like making the effort before you arrived.' She yawned. 'Tonight I'm going to bed early with a book, and tomorrow I'm just going to laze about all day until it's party time.'

'Good plan. If you've no objection I'll do likewise.'

Her eyes flew to meet his at the guarded note in his voice.

'None at all,' she assured him, and grinned. 'Is this really us, Luke?'

His eyes danced. 'Hard to believe sometimes, but, yes, it's really us, and so far no bruises to show for it.'

The Harleys' villa was in the heart of the Chianti wine-growing area. Instead of taking the *autostrada* Luke drove along the *Chiantigiana*, the winding road which led through an endless vista of vineyards until they left it for the narrow track which wound itself up to the floodlit Villa Violetta. Ancient and beautiful, its rose-coloured colonnades reflected in the pool which had been so carefully constructed to blend with the villa's antiquity, it looked almost unreal, like a backdrop for one of the plays Shakespeare had set in Italy.

'Goodness,' said Saskia in awe as Luke parked the Alfa-Romeo among the expensive cars already there. Music was playing and laughter floated on the air, and Luke turned to her with a smile.

'Well, little sister. We're here.'

'I should have arrived in a fairy coach,' said Saskia, her smile as crooked as his. 'Will I do, Luke? Really?'

Luke had put the hood up on the car for the drive, in deference to Saskia's hair, and in the small, confined space his eyes gave her a long, leisurely scrutiny from the burnished, gold-tipped hair, down over the face she'd taken such care with, to the bare, tanned shoulders above the black chiffon, then he leaned forward and kissed her cheek. 'You look ravishing, Sassy.'

She breathed out, smiling in gratitude. 'You look pretty gorgeous yourself, brother dear.'

Luke helped her from the car with ceremony, his lips twitching at the generous length of black silk leg Saskia couldn't avoid displaying before he pulled her to her feet.

'This underslip thing is a bit narrow for getting out of cars like this,' she muttered, her face hot.

'Next time I'll bring the Rolls,' he promised. 'Come on, Cinderella. Time to meet our hosts.'

Any fears Saskia might have had about being overdressed vanished at the sight of Lauren Harley, who was a long-stemmed American beauty sheathed in white satin which left one tanned shoulder bare.

'Armani,' whispered Saskia, and Luke grinned as he took her hand and led her to join the knot of people clustered round their hosts. The rest of the guests were distributed around the pool, highlighted by lamps placed to great effect among the shrubs and trees.

Tom Harley was very tall, with fair hair bleached by the Californian sun. As he caught sight of the new arrivals his tanned face lit with a wide white grin and he came loping towards them, arms outstretched, to give Luke an affectionate hug.

'Luke, old buddy, great to see you,' he cried, clapping him on the shoulder.

'Likewise, Tom,' said Luke, smiling. 'Saskia, this is our host. Tom, meet my little sister.'

Tom took Saskia's hand, his face blank for a moment, then his eyes narrowed at Luke. 'That Brit sense of humour again?' He grinned down into Saskia's face. 'We had cola and cookies waiting for you, honey. We thought Luke was bringing a baby, not a babe.'

Saskia laughed, and shook the American's large hand. 'Luke likes his little joke. I hope I'm not a disappointment.'

'Anything but, Saskia. Great name. Come and meet Lauren and the others. You know most people, Luke,' he said over his shoulder, and put an arm round Saskia's waist. 'I'll introduce the little sister.'

Lauren Harley was as warm and welcoming as her husband, teasing Luke for his little deception as he kissed her. She beckoned to a waiter to bring a tray of drinks.

'Grab a glass and go circulate, Luke Armytage. We'll see that Saskia meets everybody.'

'I don't know that I ought to do that. The family expects me to take great care of her,' said Luke, the smile more crooked than usual as Saskia gave him a glittering look.

'Don't worry,' she said lightly. 'Go and enjoy yourself. I'll be fine.'

He gave her a slight, formal bow, his eyes glittering in response. 'As you wish, Sassy.'

'Sassy?' said Tom, chuckling. 'Is that what people call you?'

'No. Only me,' said Luke deliberately. 'See you later.'

The moment he turned away he was embraced by a beautiful brunette in a white dress which hung precariously from two narrow straps back and front, leaving her ribs bare at the sides, before a diamanté buckle held everything together at the hips.

'Luca!' she said in a husky voice, eyes alight with pleasure, and poured a flood of liquid Italian into his ear as she kissed him on both cheeks.

'I guess that's Luke taken care of for a while,' said Lauren, and took Saskia by the hand. 'Everybody's here now, so come and meet people.'

With the Harleys either side of her, Saskia was introduced to a bewildering array of people of several nationalities—the men, in most cases, wearing suits with labels as famous as those on the feminine creations Saskia recognised from glossy magazines, as well as the trip to Florence. All the guests, in some way or other, seemed to be involved with wine, either growing grapes, making wine, selling it or writing about it. Smiling incessantly, shaking hands, trying to memorise names, Saskia circulated with the Harleys until at last a servant called Lauren away, and Tom left her with one of the younger groups of people, all of them local.

Her Italian—both taught at her grandmother's knee and studied in college—was fluent, so she was able to hold her own with the privileged young of the local wine gentry. They were all very friendly—one of them, a very good-looking young man, particularly attentive.

'I am Dante Fortinari,' he said in English after a while as he secured another glass of champagne for her. 'You must find it hard to remember so many names given to you all at once.'

She smiled, rather taken by the young man who, if he had been wearing late-fifteenth-century costume, would have blended with ease into a painting by Raphael.

Dante returned the smile, blue eyes gleaming. 'So you are Luke Armytage's sister. You are very like him. Except that you are much, much more beautiful, of course.'

Saskia thanked him for the compliment, searching for the right word. 'Actually I'm Luke's *sorellastra*—his stepsister.'

'Ah, I see.' He smiled, edging her away from the rest of the group. 'Tell me about yourself, Saskia. Do you live in London? What do you do there?' He lifted her left hand. 'No ring. No *fidanzato*?'

'Which question shall I answer first?' she retorted, smiling.

'The last one,' he said promptly.

Saskia disengaged her hand gently. 'No fiancé. I work in a merchant bank, where my Italian—and French—comes in handy, and I live alone in a flat in Chiswick.' But she didn't have a flat in Chiswick for the time being, she reminded herself. She shivered suddenly, aware of a cool breeze on her bare shoulders.

'Come,' said Dante instantly. 'You are cold, and our hostess beckons. We must go inside for supper. May I have the pleasure of your company for the meal, Miss Saskia Ford?'

'Of course.'

When she mounted the steps to the terrace, careful in her new shoes, she found Luke standing still at the top, waiting for them.

'Your big brother is looking for you,' said Dante, smiling. '*Come stai*, Luke? Do not worry for Saskia; I am taking her into supper.'

'Hello, Dante.' Luke slid an arm round Saskia's waist as she reached him. 'Is that all right with you, Sassy?'

'Of course.' She detached herself, smiling. 'You run along and enjoy yourself, brother, dear. Dante here has promised to look out for me.'

'Right.' Luke gave the dark, elegant young man a straight look. 'Take good care of her, Dante.'

The young Italian bowed gracefully. 'It will be my privilege.'

The dining room was full of small tables, with a large buffet supper laid out at one end for guests to help themselves from the wonderful array of food. Once their plates were filled Dante led Saskia to a table where some of the group from the garden were saving seats for them. They were a convivial, friendly crowd, with faultless manners to the stranger in their midst, as they questioned Saskia about her life in London, and about Luke.

'He is so charming,' sighed one of the girls. 'Does he have a special lady in London, Saskia?'

'Not at the moment. But that won't last long, I'm sure.'

'I am sure, too,' said Dante quickly. 'All women adore Luke. But take no notice of Mirella; she has always had a crush on him, ever since he came first to do business with our father. It is a pity he did not bring you here, last month, to the Rassegna del Chianti Classico, the big festival of local wines. You would have enjoyed that.'

'I'm sure I would.'

Of course, thought Saskia, enlightened. Fortinari—one of the oldest names in wine-making, and the most respected. Dante and Mirella must be sprigs on the formidable family tree.

When the meal was over Tom gave a graceful speech, half in English, half in creditable Italian, thanking the guests for coming to mark another safe harvest of what looked like being a very good year for his wine. He was given a cheer by people who obviously liked him, even though in some ways he was a fair way to beating them at their own game with the introduction of new blends of grape to mix with the traditional Sangiovese vine, grown in this part of the world for centuries.

Tom was a good raconteur and everyone enjoyed his speech, including Luke, who was at the same table as his hosts, accompanied by the brunette in the precarious white dress.

Afterwards coffee was served on the terrace, accompanied by brandy or Vin Santo, according to taste. When Dante ushered Saskia outside Luke came to join them.

'Enjoy your supper?' he asked as they sipped the strong black coffee no Italian could exist without for long.

'Delicious.' She waved an arm, beckoning to Mirella, whose eyes lit up like lamps at the sight of Luke. 'I believe you know Mirella Fortinari?'

Luke took the girl's hand, smiling warmly. 'Of course; how are you? When I came last you were in college.'

'I know,' she said, returning the smile with interest. 'I missed you.'

As Saskia watched Mirella's big dark eyes trained worshipfully on Luke's she was conscious of a strange sensation deep inside her, similar to the pang she'd felt when the siren in the Gucci dress had appropriated Luke earlier on.

She came back to earth as Dante asked if she would like to dance, only now noticing that music had started in the quickly cleared dining room.

'Yes,' she said, pulling herself together to give him a radiant smile. 'If you'll give me five minutes to tidy up, I'd love to dance.'

After a moment to collect comb and lipstick from Luke's inside pocket, Saskia was shown to a bathroom straight out of the *Arabian Nights'*, and took time to coax her hair into place and renew her lipstick, secure in the knowledge that tonight she'd never looked better in her life. Amazing what fine feathers can do, she told her reflection. As she was leaving the bathroom she met her hostess, who was anxious to confirm that Saskia was enjoying herself.

'It's a wonderful party, Lauren. I'm having the time of my life,' she assured her, and went down to join the others. Luke's tawny head stood out from the rest in the crowded room as he danced with Mirella Fortinari, who looked quite dazed with pleasure at the experience.

Dante Fortinari, who was waiting for Saskia at the door, was a reasonably tall man, but Saskia measured five feet eight inches in her bare feet, so that in the new shoes she'd bought in Florence she was on eye level with her partner as they danced to the old Cole Porter standards which were Tom Harley's favourites.

'You dance well,' said Dante in the husky, deep voice characteristic of so many Italian men.

'I learnt in school,' she said, smiling. 'But I don't have much practice these days. We just sort of jig about to pop music at parties at home.'

'We do here, also,' he assured her, and smiled, his oval, heavy-lidded eyes gleaming. 'But it is good to hold a beautiful woman in one's arms. I like Tom's music.'

Saskia liked it, too. But something was missing. Dante was a charming, likeable man, but somehow she felt that the dress, the occasion, required more—the touch of enchantment that came from dancing with someone special. Francis, perhaps?

'Why do you shake your head?' asked Dante softly.

Saskia smiled at him in apology. 'I didn't know I was doing it.'

A break in the music sent them from the floor to join Mirella and Luke and the group Saskia and Dante had joined for supper.

'Where's the lady in the white dress?' Saskia said to Luke in an undertone, giving him the lipstick and comb to stow away.

'Her husband arrived during supper,' he said out of the corner of his mouth. 'Didn't you notice?'

'No.' Which was the truth. Saskia had purposefully kept her eyes from Luke during the meal.

'Hello, Armytage,' said a new voice, and Luke turned to greet a man with wiry black hair and sharp features, introducing him as Joel Gilbert, wine writer and journalist.

Dante, who already knew him, made punctilious introductions all round, after which Joel turned to Saskia with an appraising look.

'Luke's kept you a dark secret, Saskia. I never knew he had a sister.'

'Stepsister,' she corrected.

'You're very alike.'

'The resemblance is pure coincidence,' said Luke rather coolly, winning a surprised look from Saskia.

'The music's started up,' said the newcomer. 'Will you dance with me, Saskia?'

Neither Dante nor Luke looked very pleased as the journalist led Saskia onto the floor to the strains of a smoochy Peggy Lee record.

'I keep thinking I've met you before,' said Joel as he held her rather more tightly than she cared for.

'I don't think so.'

'I never forget a face. It will come to me. Where are you staying? In Florence?'

'No. My family have a house not too far away from here.'

'Whereabouts?'

'A few kilometres from San Gimignano.'

'Are you here on holiday?' he asked, and when she replied in the affirmative went on to fire questions about her life in London. Suddenly he snapped his fingers. 'Got it! I saw you at Ascot with the heir apparent to the Lawford restaurant group. Aren't you the lady helping Francis recover from his divorce?'

'No. Just a friend.' Saskia cut the catechism short. 'That's enough about me. Tell me about your life, Joel; it sounds a lot more interesting than mine.'

It was a ploy which rarely failed to work. Most men were only too eager to give Saskia every last detail, whether she was interested or not. By the time the music stopped she'd learned that Joel had been in journalism since he was a boy, enjoyed visiting the various major vineyards as part of his job, that he'd appeared on television in a programme about wine, and supported Chelsea football team.

'Goodness,' said Saskia with mock sympathy. 'Ah, well, someone has to.'

'That's fighting talk,' he chuckled as they rejoined the others. 'Thank you for the dance. Give me your number in London later.'

Saskia smiled noncommittally, glad when the Harleys joined them and the band took a rest to give way to some old Bill Haley records.

'Are you too young to remember this one, Saskia?' said Tom, seizing her hand. 'Let's rock and roll, baby!'

Laughing, Saskia followed him to the centre of the floor where he began to throw her around in perfect rhythm to the music, their feet combining in time to the irresistible beat.

Her hair was flying as Tom spun her away from him then back again, her face glowing as the rest of the guests formed a circle round the room, urging them on. She caught sight of Luke's astonished face as he watched her, then forgot him in her concentration on keeping up with her partner, who twirled her round him like a matador with a cape. As the music came to a climax Tom tossed her up into the air, caught her exactly on the beat, and set her down, holding her hand as he bowed to the audience, who were applauding wildly.

'Your baby sister is one hell of a dancer,' panted Tom as he took Saskia back to the others.

'So I see,' said Luke, eyeing Saskia blankly.

'Do you mean you've never danced with her?' demanded Lauren, laughing.

'Er-no.' Luke looked oddly embarrassed.

'We don't see each other that much,' said Saskia, still out of breath.

'Why not?' asked Dante Fortinari, deeply interested.

Luke shrugged. 'Until recently Saskia was very much involved with someone. She had no time to spare for mere stepbrothers.'

Dante nodded. 'It is only natural that a lover would wish to monopolise her. Are there more of you?' he added with interest.

'If you mean do I have another stepsister like Saskia, no,' Luke said, grinning. 'The others are three-year-old twin boys.' He looked up as slower music began. 'Right, then, Saskia, never let it be said that Tom Harley beat me at anything. Let's dance.'

It was strange, she thought as he took her in his arms, that each of her partners had a very different style. Dante had held her respectfully, but with unconcealed pleasure, Joel Gilbert had gripped her much too tightly for comfort, and Tom had involved her in something not far short of a cabaret act. But Luke was different. He held her in an oddly impersonal way. He wasn't even all that wonderful a dancer. But she found she was enjoying herself with him far more than the others.

'You're leading,' he said dryly at one point.

'Sorry. I always had to be the man in school because I'm tall.' Saskia smiled up at him, surprising an odd look in his eyes.

'Anything less like a man than you tonight would be hard to imagine,' he said gruffly, and held her closer.

They finished the dance in silence, then returned to the teasing of the others.

'Looked pretty painless to me,' commented Tom. 'Did he tread on your toes, Saskia?'

'Certainly not,' said Luke promptly. 'If anything the boot was on the other foot.'

'I did not step on your toes,' Saskia retorted, secretly rather grateful that Luke had played up the brother/sister angle by insulting her. Because something in the way Joel Gilbert had been watching them as they left the dance floor bothered her. She didn't like him, she decided, which was silly. Apart from a tendency to hold her too close, he had been pleasant enough.

During the following hour both Saskia and Luke danced with a succession of partners, but not again with each other. She partnered Joel Gilbert again, with concealed reluctance, and had a more conventional dance with Tom, but Dante Fortinari danced with her most. It was late and she was tired when Luke intercepted her as she came off the dance floor.

'Just tell me when you want to go home,' he said as Dante went off to look for his sister.

'Whenever you like.' She smiled at Luke, stifling a yawn. 'At one time I could dance all night then get up and work a full day. Am I getting past it at twenty-five, Lucius Armytage?'

'Of course not. It's nearly three in the morning, Sassy. You're entitled to feel tired.'

'How about you?' she said, frowning. 'You still have to drive home.'

'I've just had some coffee with Lauren, while you were dancing with Dante, and I've had very little to drink. I promise to get you home safely.'

'I wasn't thinking of that,' she protested. 'I meant you must be tired.'

His eyes softened. 'I keep forgetting this is the new you. But don't worry; it's not far. I know the road well, and it's a beautiful night.'

Saskia went with him to thank Lauren and Tom for one of the best evenings she'd ever had.

'Bring her again to celebrate next years' *vendemmia*,' said Lauren promptly.

'Just make sure Tom gets his grapes in on time, then,' begged Luke. 'Every year I'm a nervous wreck about this time, until I hear he's pulled it off again.'

Tom tapped his nose, winking. 'This tells me when.'

'What happened a few years back, then?' retorted Luke.

'I had a cold,' said Tom, with dignity, and kissed Saskia on both cheeks. 'Nice to meet you, baby sister. And don't wait until next year to visit. Get Luke to bring you to Napa Valley.'

'Come any time,' urged Lauren. She looked up at her husband with a questioning smile he answered by putting an arm round her and drawing her close. She smiled at the others radiantly. 'We haven't told anyone else—but by then, God willing, we'll have another Harley to meet you.'

Tom grinned widely as Luke wrung his hand and kissed Lauren, while Saskia, taken aback by a sharp pang of envy, added her congratulations.

'So that's why you chose Saskia to throw round the floor tonight,' said Luke, laughing.

Tom nodded. 'That's right. You shake a mean leg, Miss Saskia.'

The leavetaking was prolonged as Luke made the rounds with Saskia in tow. When they came to Mirella and Dante Fortinari, the girl looked up at Luke wistfully.

'Promise to visit us when I am at home next time?' she said.

He smiled and bent to kiss her on both cheeks. 'I promise,' he said, then shook Dante's hand. 'I look forward to receiving the next shipment.'

'It was good to see you again, Luca.' The young man turned to Saskia and took the hand she offered, kissing it gracefully. 'It was an even greater pleasure to meet his sister.'

'Stepsister,' she said automatically, and he smiled, giving her a formal little bow, as Luke took Saskia by the arm and led her from the room.

# CHAPTER SIX

THE autumn night was chilly as they walked to the car. Luke took off his jacket and put it round Saskia's bare shoulders.

'The car will soon warm up,' he said as he started the engine.

'I'm not really cold.' She gave him a smile. 'I've had too much exercise for that. I haven't danced as much for years.'

'Did you enjoy it?' he asked as the car began to glide away down the floodlit bends from the villa.

'It was quite wonderful. I like Lauren and Tom. It was a magical evening all round.'

'You were certainly the belle of the ball. Were you happy with your dress once you saw the others?'

'Very. Luke, I now realise that you knew very well what sort of party it would be. Thank you for buying me the dress. It was pretty modest—in price and cut—compared with some of the creations there tonight. Particularly the white number your friend was keeping on by some form of remote control.'

Luke chuckled. 'Luisa's husband has a lot of money. She probably won't wear the dress again. Which is just as well. Something extreme like that will be out of fashion by the next party.'

'I didn't see you dancing with her,' commented Saskia, then bit her lip, hoping Luke wouldn't assume she'd been watching his every move all night. Which she hadn't. Not *all* night.

'I didn't dare,' he said with feeling. 'That was a very worrying dress. I wasn't sure what would happen if she moved about too much.'

Saskia giggled, then stretched out her legs, feeling utterly relaxed. 'Thank you for taking me there tonight, Luke. It was quite an experience. What a house!'

'It was a crumbling ruin when Tom took it over. But he's a very successful wine maker in his own right, both here and in the States, and Lauren comes from seriously old money.'

Saskia sighed. 'Some people have it all, don't they? She's even pregnant—something they were obviously both very happy about.'

'It's the one thing that wasn't easy for them. They've been married for seven years, and, I gather, for almost all of that time they've been trying for a child. Lauren's been to a succession of very expensive doctors. So tonight was a very special celebration, not just a way to mark a good wine year. To be honest,' he added, 'I didn't really know what to expect tonight. Their parties weren't on such a lavish scale in previous years. Tonight they pushed the boat out a bit.'

'So you weren't joking when you said there might be designer jeans?'

'It was a possibility. But it wouldn't have mattered. Anyone wearing jeans would have been green with envy once they laid eyes on you.'

'Why, Cap'n Butler, I do believe you're paying me a compliment,' said Saskia in a phoney Deep South accent to disguise her pleasure.

'I wasn't the only one who liked your looks. Young Dante was very taken with you.'

'He's very young. But very sweet. I liked him.'

'Dante Fortinari is a good five years older than you, Sassy.'

She laughed. 'Is he really? But it was a pleasure to be with him, however old he is. Because he knows the rules. Which is more than can be said for your friend Joel Gilbert.'

'Why?' said Luke instantly, glancing sharply at her. 'What did he do?'

'Just asked me too many questions,' she said quickly. 'He wanted my London phone number, but I told him I was flat hunting and didn't have one.'

'Very sensible. One of his chums is a gossip columnist. Joel's always on the lookout for the odd juicy titbit.'

'I can hardly be of any interest to him!'

'Possibly not. But give him a wide berth anyway.' He yawned suddenly, slowing a little. 'Not far now. I should have taken the *autostrada*, I suppose, but it seemed a shame to pass up a trip through the vineyards by starlight. Pity the moon is new. This bit of the world looks wonderful by moonlight.'

'I can well believe it,' she agreed softly.

There was silence for a while, then he cast a swift look at her face. 'Are you better now, Sassy?'

She didn't pretend to misunderstand. 'Yes. Much better.'

'I should be going back on Monday,' he said quietly. 'But, frankly, I hate the thought of leaving you at the villa on your own.'

'I would have been anyway, Luke. I'll be fine.' Which wasn't the exact truth. Without Luke for company the villa was likely to be a lonely place.

'Why not come back with me?' he suggested. 'Spend the rest of your holiday in Oxford?'

Saskia thought it over. It might be a very sensible thing to do. The trip, with Luke's help, had begun the cure for Francis. If she stayed on her own she might start feeling sorry for herself. 'I might, at that, if you can arrange a flight,' she said slowly. 'It's probably a very good idea. I need to look for somewhere to live, anyway, now I've sublet my attic.'

'I've been thinking about that,' said Luke as he turned off on to the road up to the Villa Rosa.

'Do you know of anything? I just need something to rent for a while, until my tenant moves out.'

Luke parked the car at the back of the dimly lit villa, then got out and came round the car to help her out. 'I might. Let's talk about it over a nightcap. Neither of us drank much to-night,' he said, yawning. 'I think a glass of our old friend Vin Santo, and one or two *santucci*, would give us both a good night's sleep after all that dancing, Sassy.'

Saskia had no desire to drink wine or any-thing else, but had no intention of refusing in case Luke took it as a rebuff. And she had even less desire to go to bed yet, despite her exertions. Adrenaline was still flowing from the party, and if Luke wanted to linger a while she was only too happy to linger with him, however late it was. Because tomorrow, she thought happily, there was no need to do anything.

She kicked off her shoes and curled up in a corner of the sofa in the sitting room, aware, and still secretly amazed, that the prospect of them lazing around the villa together was such a pleasant one.

'That's a funny little smile,' observed Luke as he came in with wine bottle and glasses in one hand, a dish of almond biscuits in the other. He had taken off his jacket and the handsome tie bought in Florence, and after filling their glasses he handed her a biscuit then sank down in to a chair, stretching out his legs with a sigh.

'I was lost in contemplation of doing nothing at all tomorrow,' she said, dipping her biscuit in the wine.

'Likewise,' he said with satisfaction. 'Then on Monday I must get back to the grind. Are you still of a mind to come with me?'

Saskia nodded, crunching on her biscuit. 'If possible, yes. I'll help keep Jonty and Matt amused.'

'Bring them up to town and I'll take you all to lunch at Smollensky's Balloon.'

She looked at him sharply, but Luke's eyes were closed, his glass dangling from one long hand. 'They'd like that,' she said carefully.

'Ah, but would you?' The eyes remained shut, hiding their expression from her.

'I'd have to be a miserable soul to turn down an offer of lunch complete with clowns and magicians,' she said with asperity. 'Of course I'd like it. And it would give Marina a break. Unless,' she added swiftly, 'you meant Mother and Sam to come too?'

'No. I meant the twins and you and me. A novelty for all concerned.' He opened his eyes to give her a questioning look.

'Good idea.' Saskia met the look squarely, to convince him she meant what she said, and Luke got up, proffering the wine bottle. 'No, thanks,' she said decisively. 'Any more and I'll be telling you the story of my life. Which would be a terrible bore since you know most of it already—and rather more of one incident than anyone else does.'

'Don't worry. No one else will hear anything about it from me,' he assured her, and resumed his chair. 'Though just this once, before we dismiss the subject for good, I want you to know that in my opinion Francis Lawford is one stupid bloody fool. What the devil he thought he was doing, playing games with the ex when he'd persuaded you to move in with him, I fail to see. The man's an idiot.'

Saskia smiled at him radiantly. 'Thank you, Luke. You know just how to comfort a girl.'

He nodded complacently. 'So I'm told.'

At one time Saskia would have wanted to hit him, but now the deliberately smug look on his face merely made her laugh. 'Such conceit!'

'I was joking, Sassy,' he said quietly.

'I know,' she answered in kind.

'And that's the difference, isn't it? You don't flare up any more when I tease.'

She nodded, a smile as crooked as his curving her mouth. 'Could it be I've grown up at last?'

'Whichever way I answer that I'm in trouble!'

Saskia laughed, wriggling down until she was lying full-length on the sofa, her head propped up on a cushion. 'No. Not any more. At least, not from me.' She pushed her hair back from her face. 'Though, to be frank, if anyone had told me last week I'd be sitting here with you like this, and perfectly happy about it, I'd have laughed them out of court.'

Luke nodded, smiling his crooked smile. 'This time I'll risk admitting I feel the same. Which brings me to the subject of your accommodation problem.'

'Do you know of anything fairly cheap?' She pulled a face. 'I need to save hard so I can give in my notice at the bank in the not too distant future.'

'But would you be happy doing something less demanding?'

'If it meant shorter hours and less hassle, yes, I would.'

'Then I'll keep my ear to the ground.' He sat upright, his eyes on the hands clasped between his knees. 'With regard to a place to live, Sassy, I know of something very cheap indeed, no references needed.'

'Where?' she demanded, sitting up in turn. She swung her legs to the ground, and leaned forward. 'Near you?'

He nodded. 'Which, of course, might be the snag where you're concerned.'

'It might have been at one time,' she admitted frankly, and smiled. 'But now we've proved we can stay under the same roof without bloodshed I think I can hack it as a mere neighbour. So what and where is it, this place near you? A flat?'

He raised his head to look her in the eye. 'No. I'm suggesting you move in with me, rent-free, for a while. You said you wanted to save.'

Saskia stared at him blankly. 'You mean come and live in your new house?'

'Just until your tenant moves out. Or until we come to blows. Whichever happens soonest.' He shrugged. 'It's a fair-sized house. I've commandeered one bedroom and bathroom for myself, obviously. But you could have your pick otherwise.' He looked at her astonished face in silence. 'Are you ever going to say anything, Sassy? Your mouth's hanging open.'

She closed it with a snap, looking at him doubtfully. 'Do you *mean* this, Luke?' she said hesitantly. 'Apart from various other considerations, wouldn't I be—well—rather in the way sometimes?'

'When, exactly?' he enquired affably.

Saskia eyed him balefully. 'When you say "Your place or mine?" and the lady chooses yours, Lucius Armytage. As you know perfectly well.'

'Is that the only obstacle?'

'I'm sure there are others, but it did rather leap to mind!'

Luke got up, held out his hand, and Saskia put hers into it, letting him pull her to her feet. He took her by the shoulders, his hands warm on her bare skin as he looked down into her eyes, his own very direct.

'At the moment there are no women in my life other than Marina and you,' he informed her evenly. 'If, however, such a contingency should arise, I would make it plain that my house was out of bounds while you occupied part of it. Should you consent to do so, that is. Two relatives sharing a house is not exactly front-page news, Sassy. No one would be surprised.'

'Except me!' She grinned suddenly. 'And Sam and Mother would probably collapse in each other's arms in shock at the news.'

Luke chuckled. 'You're probably right. Anyway, it's only a suggestion. Sleep on it and let me know tomorrow. If the answer's yes I need to make a few purchases pretty quickly.' He bent, and surprised her with a swift kiss on both cheeks. 'Now, do you want to go to bed, or shall I be too noble for words and volunteer to make you some tea? But before I do there's one more thing. If the answer's no I shan't be offended, Sassy. So no more daggers drawn and all that. Speaking personally, I very much prefer the new, friendly state of affairs between us to the old hostilities.'

'So do I,' she said breathlessly, still all at sea from the caress. Then she gave him a sudden, mischievous grin. 'Besides, if I start snarling at you again you might want the dress back.'

'Keep that in mind,' he advised. 'So. Do you want some tea?'

'Yes, please, but I can make it—'

'No.' Gently he pushed her back down onto the sofa. 'Just for tonight, Cinderella, I'll make it. Though be warned—this service is not included if you do come to live in my house. I shall provide you with your own kettle!'

Saskia laughed as he left the room, and stretched out again, swinging her legs up on the sofa. Live with Luke? She thought about it at great length, trying to come to terms with the fact that it was a very tempting prospect indeed, far more than she cared to let Luke know. And rent-free, at that. She would say yes the moment he came back.

She yawned, her eyelids suddenly like lead, and she blinked them hard, hoping Luke wouldn't be long with the tea. She burrowed her head into the cushions, suddenly so tired it was an effort to keep her eyes open…

# CHAPTER SEVEN

SASKIA woke slowly in her own bed to broad daylight, and found half the day gone. And her new dress hanging on the wardrobe facing her. In sudden panic she flung back the bedclothes, relieved to find she was still wearing the black silk teddy of the night before, and even her stockings. She blew out her scarlet cheeks, leapt from the bed, stripped off the underwear, then huddled into her towelling robe for an urgent visit to the bathroom, praying she would make it there and back unseen.

Mission accomplished, Saskia raced back to her room to remove last night's make-up from her flushed face, then she slapped moisturiser onto her skin and brushed her hair, grateful now for the expensive haircut which fell so obediently into place. Thanking her lucky stars that she'd avoided meeting Luke until she looked rather more appetising, she pulled on a shirt and jeans, then stood still, dismayed to hear voices somewhere outside, followed by a tap on her door.

'Sassy,' called Luke softly. 'Are you awake?'

'Just about.'

'We've got company.'

She grimaced, unseen. 'Who is it?'

'Dante and Mirella. I'm giving them coffee in the kitchen. It's a bit chilly and grey out there today. You need a sweater.'

Saskia took time to make up her face, then hunted out the long cardigan she'd had no need of until now. Woven from the wool of some northerly Scottish sheep, and dyed a shade of burnt orange that went well with the gold threads in her hair, it was a comfort against the sudden cold of the day. She found a lipstick that toned, tied a white-dotted green cotton scarf at her throat, and went out to meet the visitors.

Dante and Luke got up from the table as she entered the kitchen, the former coming forward, hand outstretched. Luke smiled at her, the familiar teasing gleam in his eyes.

Mirella smiled shyly. 'I hope we did not wake you, Saskia. We brought you this.' She gestured towards a small gilt evening purse on the table. 'I thought it might be yours.'

Saskia smiled warmly at the girl, and shook hands with Dante, who, like Luke, was dressed in jeans and sweater, with a glove-thin suede jacket slung over the back of his chair.

'I hope you are not exhausted,' he said, holding onto her hand a little longer than strictly necessary.

'Not in the least. I've been sleeping for hours. Good morning, everyone.' Saskia smiled at Luke, who placed a cup of coffee beside the empty place at the table and held out a chair for her, surprising her with a casual kiss on her cheek as she sat down.

''Morning, sleepyhead. Dante and Mirella came round to ask us out to lunch.'

'How nice,' lied Saskia, resisting an urge to touch her hand to her cheek. 'It was very kind of you to trouble to bring the purse, but it isn't mine.' Because her only handbag was a large, all-purpose affair, she had dispensed with one altogether the night before.

'Then we shall take it back.' Mirella cast an eye at Luke, then looked at Saskia pleadingly. 'You will come out to lunch? Please?'

Saskia hadn't the heart to refuse. Mirella, it was fairly obvious, had manufactured the excuse of the purse to achieve another meeting with Luke. Though, to be fair, Dante was equally pressing. She looked at Luke. 'All right with you?'

He nodded. 'But we can't stay out too long. At least, I can't. I've got some work to do this evening before I fly back tomorrow.'

'You are leaving tomorrow?' said Mirella, looking stricken.

'He'll be back,' said Dante, grinning, then looked at Saskia. 'Will you be back also?'

'She comes here a lot,' said Luke blandly. 'This house belongs to her mother—my charming stepmother,' he added. 'Marina allows me to come and go here as I need to.'

'You are fond of her,' stated Dante, and looked at Saskia. 'If the lady is as beautiful as her daughter it is not difficult to see why.'

'Oh, she is,' said Luke. 'Though in a totally different way. Sassy gets her looks from her father's family.'

Dante smiled at Saskia. 'Does everyone call you Sassy in England?'

'No. Only the twins. And Luke keeps it up to annoy me.' Saskia got up to get the coffee pot from the stove. 'Refill, anyone?'

Eventually it was decided to lunch in a *trattoria* well-known to the Fortinaris, but the journey was made in separate cars, since Luke made it clear that he could spare only a couple of hours for lunch as he had work to do later. Saskia, he said blandly, could linger over lunch rather longer if she wished.

Dante smiled. 'But you are not returning to England tomorrow, of course, Saskia. You told me last night that you were here for another week.'

'She's changed her mind. She's coming back with me,' said Luke firmly. 'But you can drive Saskia to the restaurant, Dante,' he added, with the air of one granting a great favour. 'I shall take Mirella with me. If that's all right with you, Sassy?' he added, putting a hand on her wrist as she passed him.

She gave him a feline little smile. 'Oh, yes, brother, dear. Anything you say.'

\* \* \*

The short journey to the *trattoria* was accomplished in a terrifyingly short time in Dante's Ferrari. The young Italian, talking animatedly all the way, drove as though the devil were on his tail, and had established Saskia at a table and provided her with a drink by the time the others arrived.

'You must have flown here,' said Luke, eyeing Saskia's pallor.

Saskia, incapable of speech, could only nod before downing half a glass of mineral water in one swallow.

'He drives too fast,' said Mirella, shaking a finger at her brother. 'You have frightened Saskia.'

Dante shrugged, unrepentant, a distinct swagger in his manner as he seated himself close to Saskia. 'I drive well. There was little traffic on the road, therefore no danger.'

The meal was good, and the company entertaining, but when two hours were up Luke looked at his watch and rose, deaf to the entreaties from both the Fortinaris. 'No. Pleasant as this is, we must go. Are you coming back with me, Sassy?'

She nodded with alacrity, and expressed her thanks to Dante, but refused his offer to take her for a drive before delivering her back to the villa later. 'It was so nice to meet you both. Perhaps we can do this again some time.'

'If you will give me your telephone number,' said Dante persuasively, 'I will contact you in London. I go over several times a year. We could have dinner together, yes?'

'At the moment she doesn't have a telephone number,' said Luke, taking the words out of Saskia's mouth. 'She's flat hunting.'

Dante's bright blue eyes looked from one tall tawny-haired figure to the other, then narrowed. 'Have no fear, Luca. I wish only to dine with your sister.'

'He knows that,' said Saskia hurriedly. 'But he's right. I really don't have a phone number; I've just sublet my flat to someone else.'

'Why did you do that?' asked Mirella curiously as they made their way out to the cars.

'I thought I was moving to—another flat. But it didn't happen.' Saskia smiled at Dante. 'I can give you my mother's number in Oxford. She will always pass a message on.'

'*Mille grazie,*' said Dante, and grinned at Luke while Saskia scribbled the number on an envelope. 'I could ring Luca, too, of course. But perhaps he would not allow me to know where you were.'

'I take my family responsibilities very seriously,' agreed Luke blandly.

After protracted farewells Saskia only relaxed when she was on the way back to the villa in the Alfa-Romeo.

'That,' she informed him, 'was a terrifying experience.'

'Dante's driving?' Luke glanced at her. 'I noticed you hardly touched your lunch.'

'I couldn't. My stomach was heaving with pure terror,' she said, shuddering. 'My whole life flashed before my eyes. Thank heavens he didn't propose a meal in Florence or Lucca. I'm very glad you have work to do,' she added. 'Otherwise Mirella might have persuaded you into some other jaunt after lunch.'

'I don't have any work to do.'

Saskia gave him a severe look. 'You were *lying*, Lucius Armytage?'

'Only a white lie. Just like the purse the Fortinaris brought along with the excuse that it might be yours.' Luke gave her a swift, sidelong glance. 'I would have preferred to stay at the villa today in peace. I don't know about you, but I'm tired.'

'You know perfectly well I'm tired,' she retorted. 'Which reminds me—I apologise for going to sleep on you last night.'

'When I got back with the tea tray you were dead to the world, so I put you to bed.' Luke paused. 'I didn't think you'd be pleased if I let you sleep in the dress. So I took it off. Not without difficulty, since you weren't in the least co-operative, but with great respect, I promise you. I kept my eyes averted as much as possible.'

Saskia giggled. 'And how much was that?'

'Not very much,' he admitted, then gave her the sidelong look again. 'I'm only human.'

Saskia's much tried stomach gave a disturbing lurch. The thought of Luke undressing her sent such instant heat rushing through her body that she tugged at the scarf at her throat.

'Feeling sick?' he said instantly.

'A bit,' she fibbed, and he slowed down almost to a crawl as they negotiated the bends up to the villa.

'There,' he said as he switched off the ignition. He turned to look at her. 'By the way, I was forced to interfere where Dante was concerned. The idea of his driving you round London made my blood run cold.'

Saskia shuddered. 'Mine, too—I was glad of the interference.' Which, she realised, surprised, was quite true. A week before she would have been incensed. She was tired, she decided. Not herself after such a late night.

'Come on,' said Luke, unfolding his long legs. 'Let's go in and have that tea you never managed last night.'

'I need a bath first,' she said firmly. 'I haven't recovered from sleeping in my clothes.'

'Right,' yawned Luke, stretching mightily. 'I'll have one afterwards. So no reading in the tub this time, Sassy.'

'How do you know I do that?' she said curiously.

'A certain bathroom scene is imprinted on my mind,' he informed her. 'There was an open book on the floor.'

'I refuse to let you embarrass me,' she said with dignity, and stalked off to her room for a change of clothes. But no book.

Saskia thoroughly enjoyed the restful, uneventful evening with Luke. In fact, she realised in bed later, she'd enjoyed it just as much as the glamorous party of the night before. Which no one would ever believe. She found it hard to swallow herself.

It must be the contrast. During her brief relationship with Francis, quiet evenings had been a rarity. He'd preferred dining out and clubbing, or taking her to the cinema or the theatre. Francis seemed driven to live life to the full. During the summer he had taken her to Wimbledon to watch the men's final, to the Henley Regatta, Ascot and Goodwood, even to Lord's to watch a test match. Twice she'd been forced to ask her boss for a day off to accommodate her new social whirl, something which had not gone down at all well.

Yet now all of it seemed like something in another life, far removed from lazing around doing nothing with the stepbrother who'd always rubbed her up the wrong way. Luke hadn't even asked her for a decision about moving in with him. The more she thought about it, the more she liked the idea. But it was by no means a decision to take lightly.

When Saskia arrived at the breakfast table next morning, Luke greeted her with a gloomy apology.

'I've been on the phone since the crack of dawn, but I can't get you on my flight, or any other today, I'm afraid. The earliest I could manage was Wednesday. Will that do? Or would you rather stick to your original flight next week?'

Saskia shook her head firmly. 'No. Wednesday will be fine.' She poured herself some coffee from the pot Luke had ready. 'What time do you leave?'

'Mid-morning. I need to get the car back beforehand, so I'd better allow extra time for the trip to Pisa.' He eyed her, frowning. 'I'm not very happy about leaving you here on your own. Look, I could ring the Harleys—'

'Please don't. I'll be fine. I was before you came, remember? And if you tell the Harleys I'm on my own Dante might find out and come zooming round to take me for a drive!'

'God forbid,' said Luke piously.

'Amen,' agreed Saskia. 'Now, how about some breakfast to keep you going until your plastic feast on the plane?'

'Good idea. Share it with me.'

'Have you thought any more about my suggestion?' asked Luke later as Saskia made more coffee after the meal.

She nodded, and set the pot on the table. 'Would you be offended if I asked to think about it a bit longer before I decide?'

'Not at all,' he said politely, and changed the subject to her rearranged flight and the confirmation that was necessary. 'I'll call in on Serafina on my way,' he added, 'and tell her what's happening. I'll arrange for Carlo to drive you to the airport at Pisa on Wednesday. And I'm leaving you this.' He pushed his cellphone across the table.

'I don't need that,' she said, taken aback. 'I'll just ring Mother before you go to give her the change of plan, but otherwise I quite like not having a telephone in the house.'

'I know Marina prefers it that way, but she's never been here alone, as you are. So keep it, Saskia.'

'You're very masterful all of a sudden,' she said acidly.

He shrugged, and got up, looking down at her. 'I prefer to know you can contact someone if necessary, even if it's only Serafina. You might feel ill, or the electricity might go off, or you might just fancy a chat with Marina or one of your girlfriends. You can give it back when you come home.'

'Oh, very well,' she said irritably. 'I just hope I don't lose the thing.'

'Carry it in your handbag.' He grinned suddenly. 'It must be about the only thing you don't have in there.'

She smiled back reluctantly. 'All right. But I'm a big girl, now. I'm not really an airhead, Luke.'

'Anything but. Nevertheless I just wish you weren't staying on here alone. If I didn't need to get back for a meeting tomorrow I'd suggest we switch tickets, then I could even drive you to the airport—'

'For heaven's sake, Luke, stop fussing. I was going to stay here alone for at least another week originally!'

'Pax!' He held up his long, slim hands in laughing surrender. 'I need to be off in half an hour. Let's keep to the truce until then, at least.'

When Luke was packed and everything in the car Saskia went outside with him in to the cool, misty day, secretly longing to go with him.

'Drive safely,' she said at last as Luke checked he had everything.

He turned to her, looking down at her for a moment, then gave her a quick hug and kissed her on both cheeks. '*Ciao*, Sassy. I've left a couple of paperback thrillers in the bathroom for you. And I'll tell Serafina to come up later and confirm the arrangements for Wednesday.'

Saskia, cheeks flushed, gave him a bright smile as he slid into the car. 'Thanks, Luke. See you.'

'Remember to lock up,' he ordered, and she sprang to attention, saluting cheekily.

'Yes, *sir*!'

He grinned, waved, and moments later Saskia was alone—and feeling more lonely than she would have believed possible as she wandered forlornly into the house. Just a week before the villa had felt like sanctuary when she arrived, still smarting from the humiliation of Francis. Now, without Luke, it just felt empty.

After what seemed like one of the longest days in her life, Saskia was in the kitchen, a book propped up on the coffee pot in front of her salad, when the phone rang that evening. She snatched it up, fiddling with the unfamiliar buttons for a moment, then said 'Hello?' eagerly, smiling as she heard Luke's voice.

'Hi, Sassy. I'm back in wet, windy London. Are you all right?'

'I'm fine.'

'What have you been doing with yourself?'

'Nothing much.' Saskia leaned back in her chair, hoping he wasn't in a hurry. Luke, however, seemed as happy to talk as she was, and it was a good fifteen minutes before he rang off, leaving her a lot more pleased with life. Later on, when she'd cleared away and could find nothing else to do, she allowed herself the luxury of a call to her mother, to ask Marina's advice about a temporary stay in Luke's new house.

There was silence for a time.

'I'm not sure I heard you properly,' said Marina cautiously.

'Yes, you did, Mother. Your favourite stepson asked me if I'd like a room in his house for a bit. My flat is sublet, remember?'

'I see.' Another pause. 'How do you feel about that?'

'I'm not sure. We've managed to survive a few days here at the villa together without bloodshed. Maybe it would be pushing it to share a house, even on a temporary basis. What do you think?'

'You could try it, I suppose.'

'You sound doubtful.'

'You've always avoided each other as much as possible up to now, darling. I can't quite get used to the idea of you as friends.'

'Neither can I. Nor Luke, I think. But a rent-free room is a tempting offer. And I don't think he expects me to wash his shirts in exchange.'

'The house is only half-furnished,' warned Marina.

'As long as there's a bed for me to sleep in that won't bother me.'

'Then try it. You can always move if it doesn't work out.'

'True.' Saskia changed the subject to ask about the twins and Sam, and confirmed she was returning on Wednesday. 'Though I'm not quite sure what time I'll be in Oxford. I'll ring you.'

'Where are you ringing from now, Saskia?'

'Luke left his phone with me, so I'd better say goodnight. Kiss Sam and the boys for me. See you soon.'

Saskia was not fond of flying, but after another day alone at the villa she welcomed the prospect, and the flight from Pisa was uneventful until the plane encountered bad weather over France. It arrived late at Heathrow, to make a bumpy landing in the teeth of a gale. Her knees were still trembling as she came through Customs, in no mood for a trip on the train to Reading to catch another train for Oxford.

'Carry your bag, miss?' said a familiar voice, and she looked round to see Luke grinning down into her astonished face.

Saskia beamed and threw her arms round him, and Luke bent his head involuntarily for a kiss which landed on her mouth instead of her cheek as they were jostled by passing travellers. At the unexpected contact Luke's arms tightened, and he went on kissing her, at length, with total disregard for passers-by.

He raised his head after a while, eyes gleaming. 'Welcome home, Sassy,' he said at last.

'You didn't say you were coming to meet me,' she said breathlessly, her colour high.

He hoisted her bag and took her by the arm. 'I tried to ring you all day yesterday with no success. Where the hell were you?'

'I wasn't anywhere. There must be some-thing wrong with your phone.' She fished for it in her crammed handbag while she tried to control her breathing and her thumping heart. 'There. Take the wretched thing.'

Luke examined it, lips twitching. 'You pressed the wrong button. You turned it off altogether, Sassy.'

'Oh.' Not for the world would she have let him know she'd stayed in all day, waiting for the phone call which never came. 'Sorry.'

'I assumed you were out with Dante.'

A look up at his face confirmed that the idea hadn't met with his approval. 'Would it matter if I had been?' she retorted, secretly pleased.

'You know damn well it would!'

Suddenly Saskia felt absurdly happy. She gave Luke a blazing smile as he steered her towards the taxi rank outside.

'You came by taxi?' she asked, astonished.

'No. I came on the underground.' He smiled down at her as they stood in line. 'But that plane of yours was hellishly late. You need a taxi at this stage, not a fight with the tube.'

'But I was going to Reading to catch a train for Oxford.'

His eyes held hers. 'I thought perhaps you might do that tomorrow, and stay over tonight in my place. Give it the once-over before you make up your mind about moving in. We could go out to dinner, or send out for something—whichever you like. I rang Marina to say what I had in mind, since I couldn't reach you at the villa. But you can ring her yourself once we're in the taxi. Tell her what *you* want to do.' He bundled her inside a taxi as their turn came. 'Where to, then, Sassy? Reading or my place?'

# CHAPTER EIGHT

'YOUR place,' Saskia said without hesitation, and took his phone for a brief conversation with Marina.

'There,' she said afterwards, sitting back with a sigh as they reached the motorway. 'I can't say I'm sorry to miss the journey to Oxford tonight. There was horrible turbulence over the Channel, and the plane did a sort of zig-zag down to the runway as we landed.'

'The wind's pretty high. I was worried by the time the plane came in. Some flights were cancelled.' He took her hand in his. 'Are you tired, Sassy?'

'Not really. I always feel marvellous once I've landed safely. Adrenaline, I suppose. I'm hungry, though, because I can never eat on a plane. How about you? Had a busy day? I've never really known what your business actually entails—' She stopped suddenly, conscious she was chattering. The accidental kiss, followed by the warmth of the hand holding hers, had deprived her of any remnants of poise left after the bumpy flight.

'I'll tell you all about my working day later,' he said, sounding amused. 'In the meantime don't you want to know where we're heading? You've never asked where my house actually is.'

'If Zoë turned her nose up at it I assume it's in the back of beyond somewhere.'

'Certainly not. I live in west London, not far from the Uxbridge Road, and conveniently near the M4, which is handy for visits to Oxford. By the way, are you coming up again on Saturday? I've booked a table at Smollensky's Balloon, and broached it with Marina and Dad. But it hasn't been mentioned to the demon duo, in case it fell through, because I gather they've been a bit off-colour.'

'So Mother said. But they'll be fighting fit by Saturday, no doubt. I'm game if you are,' said Saskia, laughing.

When the taxi drew up in a quiet crescent of Victorian houses Saskia was surprised. The houses were attractive enough, with pretty front gardens, and were no doubt vastly expensive, but surely not desirable enough to make Luke break up with Zoë over one of them?

Luke paid off the driver, then lifted Saskia's hold-all and beckoned her to a gap between two of the houses. In the darkness, despite the street light, Saskia hadn't noticed a narrow path lined with tall hedges.

'I'll go first,' said Luke. 'Be careful. The surface is a bit rough in places. Stay close behind me.'

Deeply intrigued, Saskia zipped up her waterproof jacket and turned up her collar against the wind, following Luke's tall shape, which looked bulkier than usual in a raincoat. He led her along the tunnel-like path to a tall, wrought-iron gate at the end of it, fastened with a chain and padlock.

Luke turned a key in the lock, pushed the gate open, and security lights came on to illuminate a tiny formal garden and a house whose symmetry was its only adornment, other than the shell-shaped portico which sheltered the fanlight above the wide front door. Two tall windows, with twelve panes of glass in each, flanked the door, with three more multi-paned windows on the floor above and two dormer windows under the roof. The house was as simple as a child's drawing, and to Saskia equally delightful. Zoë, she thought with scorn, was an idiot to prefer fashionable Docklands to this little gem.

'Well?' said Luke, putting a key into the door.

'I can't believe it's here!' said Saskia, shaking her head. She gestured to the street behind them. 'That was quiet enough, when you think the Uxbridge Road isn't far away, but this is amazing—including that hidden path. Mother never mentioned that it's a sort of oasis in the middle of suburbia.' Nor, thought Saskia with sudden guilt, would she herself have listened in the past if Marina had tried to describe Luke's home.

'It looks best at night,' he warned. 'Outside it could do with a coat of paint. It's better inside.' He switched on a light in the square hall to show a gleaming wood floor with a fringed oriental rug in the middle of it.

Turning on lights as he went, Luke led her through a formal room with more gleaming floors, empty except for shelves filled with books flanking the beautiful, austere fireplace and the gilded mirror between two candle wall-lights above it. 'I bought that only recently,' he explained. 'I've been hunting auctions and sales of various kinds in odd moments, but my recent travels have put a stop to that for the time being. The study I just brought lock, stock and barrel from the flat, of course.'

He showed her a very functional, masculine room, with a modern desk and all the technology necessary for his business interests, plus a sofa and a couple of comfortable chairs, and a television. 'I had a carpet laid in here, but the floors are beautiful, so I had the others sanded down and sealed to show the natural wood. I'll buy rugs and so on as I go along.'

The dining room boasted another graceful fireplace, but was otherwise equally empty.

'I haven't got to this room yet, either,' explained Luke. 'My other stuff is too modern, so I put it in the kitchen, which is down these stairs on a different level.'

The basement kitchen ran across the width of the house at the back, with tall windows which looked out onto a paved courtyard area with a garage beyond, which, he told her, was his normal means of entry.

'But tonight I wanted to impress you by coming along my own private front path.' Luke pointed out the cooker and the central island with the designer sink and electric hobs, which, like the bathrooms upstairs, had been installed by the previous owner. Finally he opened a door to an old-fashioned pantry and revealed a washing machine and a refrigerator, then stood with arms folded, looking at her quizzically. 'Well? Do you want to turn tail and run? Or do you fancy a look upstairs?'

Saskia slid out of her damp jacket and put it over the back of a chair. 'Are you kidding? Of course I do.'

Luke led her back to the hall, and on up the staircase to a landing which branched to divide the upper floor neatly into two halves, with a long window at the head of the stairs looking down on the courtyard at the back. On one side of the landing Luke's bedroom, austerely com-

fortable with carpet and furniture from his previous flat, connected with a luxuriously fitted
bathroom. Beyond it lay another small, empty
bedroom with bare boards.

Luke raised an eyebrow. 'Now for the acid
test.'

Across the landing two rooms were connected by a bathroom with a claw-foot tub
standing against a mirror-lined wall. One bedroom held bunk-beds and a small wardrobe,
the other a tall, mahogany cheval mirror and a
large bed with a headboard fashioned of intri-
cately carved brass.

Saskia gazed at the room in silence, then
looked up at Luke. 'This is lovely. Utterly
lovely. Are you sure you want me to have it?
You could let it for heaven knows what to a
paying tenant.'

'Maybe I will. Eventually. I'd rather get the
house finished first.'

'How long have you actually lived here?'
she asked curiously. 'I didn't take much notice
when Mother told me you'd moved.' And had
feigned lack of interest, she thought ruefully,
at any mention of Luke's new house.

'Six months or so. Though I spend so much time travelling, I've literally slept here for only half of that. I stay put from now on, of course, until spring.' He raised an eyebrow. 'So. Are you interested? The twins love the place, hence the bunk-beds. I put Dad and Marina in my room when they stop over, and I doss down on the brass bed.' He smiled crookedly. 'You're the only one who's kept away.'

'My time was rather taken up until recently. Not,' she added tartly, 'that I've ever been invited.'

'I'm inviting you now.'

She looked at him in silence for a moment, deciding not to tell him that just one look had been enough for her to fall in love with the house. 'All right, then. Thank you. I'd like to stay. Just until my place is free, of course.'

Luke gave her his usual crooked smile. 'Of course! What a polite little sister you are, to be sure.'

'Only I'm not your sister,' she said, her eyes falling.

The smile vanished. 'For which I'm grateful—as I demonstrated so unexpectedly at the airport. But you needn't worry on that score, Sassy. It was an accident. I'll try not to make it a habit.'

'Do you usually kiss girls by accident?' asked Saskia, raising her head.

'No.'

Their eyes met, and held for a moment, then Luke turned away. 'I need a shower. Have a bath, if you feel like it. I'll bring your bag up. Would you like to go out for a meal later?'

She shook her head. 'Could we just order in something? I'm still recovering from my flight.'

'Whatever you fancy.' He yawned suddenly. 'Sorry. It's been a bit of a wrench to get back to the grind after my travels. Back to earth with a vengeance.'

'With a trip to Heathrow at rush hour to top it off.' She smiled. 'It was very sweet of you to bother.'

'Sassy, I am rarely *sweet*,' he said dryly. 'But it seemed a good opportunity to show you the house. I thought you might prefer it to a trip to Oxford.'

'I did. Thank you. I appreciate it.'

'Then don't read an entire novel in the bath. I'm hungry.'

When they met half an hour later in the kitchen, Luke was loud with approval.

'You were quick, Sassy. Wonderful. So what shall we have for our takeaway supper? The Uxbridge Road can provide food in most languages.'

She grinned at him, pushing her fingers through her damp hair. 'Would you groan if I said I fancied a pizza?'

He laughed, shrugging. 'Why not? Mrs B has done some shopping for me, so I can even rustle up a salad to go with it.'

They sat at the kitchen table later, sharing a vast four-seasons pizza, accompanied by some fruity red wine with the elegant Fortinari label. Afterwards they took coffee up to Luke's study, and Saskia listened, fascinated, while he described the vast amount of work necessary at Armytage Wines for the Christmas rush.

'So how do you feel about going back to the bank?' he asked after a while.

Saskia curled up in the chair, leaning her head back, relaxed and drowsy from the food and wine. 'Right now I hate the thought of it. But I've been in the job a long time. I might miss the cut and thrust of it all, I suppose. Though sometimes the stress factor's a bit high.' She pulled a face, and looked across at the long figure stretched out in the other chair. 'You obviously love your work.'

'I'm my own boss, remember,' he reminded her. 'Something with its own brand of built-in stress. But nothing I can't handle. You, on the other hand, sound as though you need a change.'

'I'll start looking in the papers,' she said, yawning, and smiled across at him apologetically. 'All that food and wine on top of my flight has made me sleepy. What time do you get up in the morning?'

'Crack of dawn tomorrow, alas. But you stay in bed as long as you like. Give me a ring tomorrow night to say you arrived safely in Oxford,' he added. 'Are you game to come up again on Saturday with Jonty and Matt?'

'Of course. I'll let you know what train.' Saskia frowned suddenly. 'Don't you work on Saturdays, then?'

'Sometimes. I kept this one free.' His eyes held hers. 'As I said, I'm my own boss.'

With an effort she looked away and got to her feet. 'Feeble, I know, but I'm done in. So if I'm to be fit to entertain the twins I'd better get to bed. Thanks for the meal.'

Luke uncoiled himself from the chair and strolled to open the door for her. 'My pleasure, Sassy. Do you have everything you want?'

She nodded, suddenly so much aware of his physical presence she found it hard to breathe.

There was silence for a moment, then he said abruptly, 'I don't,' and pulled her into his arms, looking down into her startled eyes. 'Earlier tonight it was an accident. This time—'

This time the kiss was different, fiercer, with a flash-fire heat that enveloped them both. Saskia's arms went round his neck, and Luke held her with rib-cracking closeness, their breath labouring in their lungs as their lips and tongues met with a passion which frightened

Saskia out of her wits and left Luke white as a sheet when he let her go at last. She backed away in silence, her eyes locked with his.

'I didn't mean that to happen,' he said hoarsely.

She took in a deep, shaky breath while the world righted itself. 'No. No, I don't suppose you did.'

Luke's eyes narrowed. 'What do you mean?'

Saskia shrugged. 'Because of the way things are.'

'Dad and Marina, you mean?'

'No.' She smiled shakily. 'I meant because you've never liked me much.'

'Saskia,' he said very clearly, '*you* were the one who hated the sight of me, not the other way round.'

'You can't pretend you were over-fond of me, Luke!'

'It's hard to be fond of a girl who spits at you like an angry cat, Sassy.' He smiled a little. 'At least that's how it used to be at first. As you grew up you were more ice maiden than spitfire.'

She returned the smile reluctantly. 'I thawed rather suddenly just now, though.'

He nodded, his eyes gleaming in appreciation. 'So what happens now?'

Saskia looked at him uncertainly. 'I'm not sure what you mean.'

'I mean,' he said deliberately, 'that now you're probably sorry you didn't go straight back to Oxford. Also that you'll start flat hunting first thing in the morning.'

'You're not casting me out into the snow tonight, then?'

He frowned. 'Sassy, I'm the transgressor, not you.'

She looked him in the eye. 'That's nonsense. It takes two, Luke.'

'I wish you'd mentioned it sooner! I wanted to make love to you in Italy. Most of the time, but especially after the party.' Luke moved closer. 'I was jealous, Sassy. I objected to watching you dance with Dante all night.'

'Not all night,' she contradicted breathlessly.

'I didn't approve of the cabaret act with Tom, either.'

'Then why didn't you dance with me more yourself, then?' she said gruffly, closing the gap between them slightly.

'Because it wasn't possible to hold you in my arms without demonstrating to the world at large that I wanted you. Badly. And I was supposed to be your brother, remember? People remarked on the resemblance.' Luke reached out his hands to take hers, his eyes glittering darkly. 'But we're not relatives, are we? Consanguinity doesn't come into it.'

She shook her head mutely.

'I would like to say I've been fond of you since the day we met, but it wouldn't be true. I always *had* looked on you as a little sister,' he went on, drawing her closer. 'Then the day I arrived at the villa I walked into the bathroom and saw a nude, breathtaking vision, like one of Canova's *Three Graces* come to life.'

Saskia smiled suddenly, her eyes dancing. 'Is that a compliment?'

His eyes closed involuntarily. 'If you're pleased because the memory keeps me awake at night, then, yes, it's a compliment. It's also the truth.' His lids lifted in a look of such blazing need her smile faded. 'But because you're Marina's daughter, and I'm my father's son, I won't do anything about it unless—'

'Unless?' she prompted.

'You feel the same way.'

Now, Saskia knew, was the time to insist that she did not—that she had no intention of getting involved with anyone for the foreseeable future after the debacle with Francis. There were all sorts of reasons why a love affair with Lucius Armytage would be sheer madness. But at the moment she couldn't think of any. The look in his eyes was making it very hard for her to think at all. And more powerful than all of that was the incredible physical response he roused in her. Something she'd never felt before for anyone.

'Luke,' she said very quietly, 'I won't lie. I do feel the same way. The time together in Italy changed us both, I know. I really loved doing the tourist things with you. And it was the same for me at the party—I was jealous of the other women you danced with. But it's all a bit sudden.'

He smiled. 'We've known each other for ten years, Sassy. It's not that sudden.'

'Feeling like this is,' she said bluntly, and disengaged her hands. 'Look, could we sit down and talk?'

'As long as you like.' He waited until she'd curled up in a chair, then sat down in the other, watching her.

'You know I had a succession of boy-friends,' she said, not looking at him. 'Your father always had lots of students in and out of the house. There was never any shortage of male company as I was growing up—randy undergraduates, most of them.'

'It used to worry Dad, I know,' said Luke. 'And I could appreciate his problem. He felt very responsible.'

Saskia's eyes softened. 'I love your father very much, you know.'

'Actually I do. It was your great redeeming feature from my point of view. Anyway, we were talking about boyfriends. Did one of them break your heart, Sassy?'

'No, nothing like that.' She shifted uncomfortably in her seat. 'Most of them were just friends. And those who wanted more than that didn't last long because—' She sighed. 'This is going to sound very far-fetched.'

'Try me.'

'I refused to play if they wanted more than kissing and touching.' She looked down at her clasped hands, her face flushed.

There was silence for a long interval, then Luke said quietly, 'Are you trying to tell me that you're a virgin, Sassy?'

She shook her head. 'During my first year in college one of Sam's students introduced me to a friend of his. Piers was very good-looking, with a double-barrelled name and a lot of charm. I fell for him in a big way, flattered by his pursuit, and utterly entranced when he invited me to the May Ball. Mother bought me a beautiful green taffeta ballgown, and off went Cinderella to dance all evening with her prince and drink champagne.

To cut the story short, I eventually found myself in Piers's room. Looking back on it, I realise he was high on more than just champagne. Before I knew what was happening, he'd pushed me onto his bed to introduce me to the sublime mystery of love—his description, not mine. It took less than two minutes, after which he sprawled on his back, snoring, and I went home.'

Luke frowned. 'But surely you didn't leave it at that?'

'It was so off-putting I left it for a long time. The other boyfriends were just that. If they were content just to be friends—and a surprising number were—fine. If not, no dice.' Saskia shrugged. 'I've had only one really close relationship since then. You met Michael Todd in Oxford, if you remember? I liked him a lot. But it ended in fiasco.'

'Reluctant though I am to bring up his name, surely Francis was more successful?' said Luke without expression.

She looked at him. 'He'd hate it if he knew I was telling you this, but I managed to postpone the acid test until I moved in with him. It was meant to be the crowning touch to our celebration that happy Saturday. Unhappily, I arrived a day early, as you know. Bad move. But up to that point I was quite sure he would be the one to change things for me. Now I'll never know.'

Luke frowned. 'Saskia, if Francis came knocking on your door tomorrow, telling you that the ex-wife was no longer part of his life, that you were the one he loved, how would you react?'

She thought about it for a moment, then shook her head. 'I wouldn't believe him. Besides, I no longer feel the same way about him.'

'Because of Amanda?'

Her eyes met his. 'No,' she said baldly. 'Because of you.'

Luke got up and pulled her to her feet, putting a finger under her chin to raise her face to his. 'Then in that case I suggest we backtrack a little. Take time to adjust to each other. I want you under my roof, whatever the sleeping arrangements—but no gentlemen callers or the deal's off.'

She grinned at him mischievously. 'Spoilsport!'

His eyes were suddenly deadly serious. 'I won't share, Saskia.'

'Neither will I!'

'Good,' he said briskly. 'Now that's sorted, I'll let you go off to bed. But because I'm letting you go alone I'll dispense with a goodnight kiss.'

Saskia smiled as she made for the door. 'Not even one little brotherly peck?'

He gave her a glittering look. 'No. As I've mentioned before, I'm only human.'

# CHAPTER NINE

SASKIA slept very little that night in the beautiful brass bed, most of it spent in regrets for her solitary state when she could have been with Luke if she'd given in to her natural instincts. But all the old doubts and fears had reared their heads at the vital moment. And this was no ordinary man-friend she could send on his way without the prospect of meeting him again—Luke was part of the family. Their relationship had never been very cordial up to now, but they were still expected to attend family functions and form part of the celebrations in Oxford at Christmas. If it all went terribly wrong, as well it might, it would make things difficult for everyone concerned.

A little after seven Saskia heard a tap on the door.

'Want some tea?' called Luke softly.

'Yes, please!' She shot upright in bed, pushing her hair back from her face, smiling as

Luke came in, elegant in a dark City suit, a cup of tea in one hand.

'Morning, Sassy. I like the nightshirt. Sleep well?'

'No,' she said frankly, and took the cup from him. 'Did you?'

'No.' He smiled at her.

'This is wonderful,' she told him, sipping blissfully, then smiled at him impudently. 'I thought this wasn't part of the Armytage service!'

'I've made an exception for your first day. Must go.' He turned in the doorway. 'Ring me tonight.'

'I will.' She hesitated. 'Thank you, Luke.'

'For the tea?'

'That, and for a great many other things, too.'

They exchanged a long look, then Luke crossed the floor and bent to kiss her cheek. 'I think I can risk this. *Ciao*, Sassy.'

Saskia arrived in Oxford to find the house in uproar because the twins had gone down with chicken pox. Her exhausted mother was delighted to see her as always, but this time had even more gratitude for her daughter's company. An extra willing hand was obviously a godsend. Life was hectic for several hours as Saskia was welcomed with open arms by two spotty, doleful little boys. She fetched drinks and did puzzles, and eventually cajoled the boys into sitting quietly to watch a cartoon video, and, because their father was away on a lecture tour in Scotland, read to them at length at bedtime to give her mother a rest.

When the little boys were finally asleep Saskia rang Luke to say the lunch at Smollensky's Balloon would have to be postponed. 'The twins came down with chicken pox overnight—simultaneously, thank heavens. This way we can at least get it over at once.'

'Poor little brats; what bad luck. How about you?' said Luke in swift concern. 'Have you had it?'

'Oh, yes. When I was their age. I've got the scars to prove it.'

'Where?'

'You mean you didn't notice at our first meeting at the villa?'

There was a pause.

'Don't say things like that,' he said huskily. 'It's bad for me.'

Another pause.

'Are you still there?' he demanded.

'Yes,' she said breathlessly. 'It's just that I'm not used to this.'

'This?'

'You know what I mean.'

'Oh, yes, Sassy. I know exactly what you mean.' He took in a deep, audible breath. 'So. When exactly do you intend moving in with me?'

Sassy slid down onto her mother's hall carpet, her back against the wall. 'I start back to the bank next Tuesday.'

'How about Sunday, then? I'll meet your train. Come early.'

'It depends what time your father arrives back. I can't leave Mother on her own with Jonty and Matt. They look so pathetic all covered in spots. And it's a terrible fight to keep them from scratching.'

'Poor little chaps—I can imagine. I'll ring tomorrow evening for a progress report. In the meantime, don't wear yourself out completely.'

'I won't. They're actually being quite good because they feel ill at the moment. But the doctor says that's likely to be short-lived. The real fun starts when they feel better.'

Luke laughed. 'I can imagine that, too. But Dad will be on hand then, and, even if I do say so myself, he's the best father in the business.'

'He certainly is!' Saskia sighed. 'A pity the twins had to miss their treat on Saturday, though. I'm sorry, too,' she added.

'So am I. Roll on Sunday.'

Saskia looked up as Marina came downstairs. 'Must go. It looks as though Mother's free to partake of something nourishing.'

'Give her my love.'

'I will.'

'Talk to you tomorrow, then. *Ciao*, Sassy.'

'That was Luke,' said Saskia, joining her mother in the kitchen.

Marina looked up from the sauce she was stirring. 'You were talking all that time to Luke?'

'Yes. I was reporting on the twins, cancelling lunch on Saturday, and so on.' Saskia perched on the table, legs swinging. 'He sent you his love. Shall I make a salad?'

Her mother nodded, looking at her searchingly. 'Are you really going to live with Luke?'

'I'm going to share his house for a while, yes.' Saskia grinned cheekily. 'There's a difference.'

'I know that. Especially as it's Luke. Throw some pasta in that pot, would you, darling?' Marina went on stirring intently for a moment. 'Francis rang a couple of times last week, by the way.'

Saskia turned sharply. 'You didn't say where I was?'

'No. Of course not. You asked me not to, remember?'

'Sorry. Anyway, what did he say?'

'Asked where you were, of course, so I said you'd gone away on holiday, and I wasn't at liberty to tell him where.' Marina's weary, beautiful eyes danced suddenly. 'He was pretty angry. All the more so, I think, because he could hardly vent his wrath on me.'

'What happened the second time?'

'Sam spoke to him.' Marina chuckled. 'He was very daunting and professorial, and made it clear he had no intention of discussing your arrangements with anyone. Francis was put very definitely in his place.'

'He must be puzzled, though,' said Saskia fairly as she drained the pasta. 'He hasn't a clue why I did a runner.'

'Are you going to tell him?'

'Only if absolutely necessary.' She pulled a face. 'I'm certainly not going to ring him up and say, "Sorry, Francis, caught you doing naughties with the wife." Smacks too much of farce.'

'Have you told Luke what happened?' asked Marina, serving the meal.

'Yes. Oddly enough he feels partly responsible—because he introduced Francis to me. Now, let's get on with this while there's peace. And by the way,' Saskia added, frowning at the shadows under her mother's eyes, 'I'll get up to see to the twins in the night, if necessary. You need a rest.'

As expected, the night was broken by demands for drinks and stories, when the two feverish, itching little boys needed comfort. And since Saskia was the next best thing to their mother she was able to settle them down each time without disturbing Marina.

The next day was not an easy one for any members of the household. Fortunately Marina's daily help was a tower of strength in seeing to shopping and even in concocting a casserole for dinner, since both Marina and Saskia had all their work cut out in looking after the twins.

Jonathan and Matthew Armytage were handsome little boys, with their father's blue eyes and their mother's dark hair, but at the moment the small faces were covered in spots, and their normal glow was dimmed. They also missed their daily, energy-channelling visit to nursery school.

'I'm sorry you can't be there, too,' said Saskia to them with feeling at one point. 'So's

Mummy. But with those spots you can't, so let's play Snakes and Ladders.'

By the evening both Marina and Saskia were weary, and heartily glad when the twins were asleep at last and looking much better.

'I hope this doesn't put you off having children of your own,' yawned Marina.

'No, of course it doesn't. Life isn't all chicken pox.'

'No. But it's pretty hectic, even when they're well. More so, sometimes.' Marina gave her daughter a sudden smile. 'Take my advice—don't leave it until you're forty-odd to have twins!'

'Do they run in Sam's family?' asked Saskia thoughtfully.

'Apparently so. Why?'

'I just hadn't heard of any in ours, that's all.' She raced into the hall as the telephone rang. 'That's probably for me.'

But when she lifted the receiver it was Sam Armytage on the line, not his son. She chatted affectionately with him, swallowing her disappointment, then fetched Marina.

While her mother was talking on the phone Saskia had a swift bath, feeling a lot better as she emerged to meet Marina coming upstairs.

'Would you mind if I just lazed around in my dressing gown tonight, Mother?'

'Good idea. I'll do the same.' Marina looked a lot more cheerful. 'Sam says he'll get away after his lecture tomorrow afternoon, instead of staying on for the dinner. Glad of the excuse, he assures me.' She stretched wearily. 'I need a bath.'

'The boys are fast asleep for the moment, so have a nice laze,' advised Saskia. 'We can eat later.'

After checking on the twins, Saskia went down to the small morning room, wondering when Luke would ring. Perhaps he worked late on Fridays. Or maybe he'd forgotten his promise to ring. Eventually convinced he was out wining and dining some woman or other, she was scowling at a television game-show when the doorbell rang. At this time of night it had to be one of Sam's students wanting help with something. In which case, she thought irritably, he or she was out of luck.

Saskia tied the girdle of her dark green robe tightly, and marched into the hall just as the front door opened and the tall figure of Luke Armytage stood there, smiling at her, key in hand.

'Luke!' she said in a choked voice hardly recognisable as her own, whereupon he closed the door behind him, dumped down a hold-all and held out his arms. She flew into them, her mouth upturned to his engulfing kiss, which confirmed, beyond any shadow of doubt, that this was really all she'd wanted since she was fifteen years old.

She slid her arms beneath his heavy rain-coat, eager to get close to him, and with a smothered sound Luke held her tightly in the crook of his arm while his free hand slid beneath the dressing gown to explore in a manner which made her knees buckle. For a long, breathless interval their absorption in each other was absolute, until at last Saskia tore herself away, face flaming as she retied her sash.

'You didn't say you were coming,' she gasped.

'I thought I might give a hand with the twins,' he said, breathing equally hard as he slid out of his raincoat. His eyes met hers. 'Or anything else you might need.'

'Marina will be delighted.'

'Good.'

'So will the twins.'

'How are they?'

'A bit better tonight. I'm so glad you came,' she added.

'I hoped you would be.'

'You know I am.'

Their eyes were telling each other so much more than the mere words that Saskia closed hers for a moment, afraid to give too much of herself away.

'Luke, I'd better go and put something on.'

He nodded, his eyes darkened almost to black as he looked her up and down from her bare feet to her tousled hair. 'Preferably right now.'

She gave him an incandescent smile, then raced up the stairs to knock on Marina's bedroom door. 'Mother, Luke's here. I thought you might want to make yourself respectable after all.'

It was a very convivial evening. The twins remained fast asleep, and the three of them were able to enjoy the casserole in peace, with the added pleasure of the wine which Luke inevitably insisted on opening to celebrate.

'What exactly *are* we celebrating, Luke?' asked Marina, looking from her flushed daughter to her tall, relaxed stepson.

'The ceasefire between Sassy and me?' he suggested, raising his glass.

'I'll drink to that,' said Saskia promptly, and her mother shook her head in wonder.

'I will, too, with the greatest of pleasure. Though I never thought I'd see the day,' she added. 'Sam will be delighted, too. Am I allowed to ask what brought the transformation about?'

Luke and Saskia exchanged glances. 'Much as I hate to say it I think I've got Francis Lawford to thank for some of it,' he said wryly.

'And maybe,' said Saskia, smiling at him, 'I just grew up at last.'

The evening passed very quickly, and Marina eventually excused herself, yawning. 'I need to go to bed. And, Luke, if you hear the boys in the night please don't show yourself. One look at you and we'll never settle them down again.'

He laughed. 'Whatever you say, Marina. I'll report for duty in the morning—try to keep them out of your hair for a bit.'

When they were alone Luke drew Saskia onto his lap on the sofa, and held her close. 'I feel an urgent need for this.'

'Likewise,' she muttered against his throat. After a while she raised her head to look into his face. 'Is this really us, or am I dreaming?'

'If you are we're sharing the same dream.' His eyes narrowed intently. 'I couldn't wait until Sunday. After I spoke to you last night I thought, Why hang about in town for the weekend when you're down here? So here I am.'

'You didn't ring to tell me.'

'I wanted to surprise you.'

'You did.'

'It was worth arriving unannounced, just to see the look on your face.'

'I was pleased,' said Saskia sedately.

He smiled triumphantly. 'I know, darling, I know.'

At the endearment they both suddenly became still, as though some boundary had been crossed. They looked at each other in silence, then, as if a question had been asked and answered, Saskia laid her head on his shoulder again.

'I've brought a present for the twins,' he said after a while.

'Good,' she said with feeling. 'We've about exhausted everything on hand.'

He chuckled. 'I can well believe it.' He shifted her in his arms more comfortably. 'Is Marina all right? She looked very tired.'

'It's only natural in the circumstances,' Saskia chuckled. 'She advised me against waiting until I'm forty-odd to have twins.'

There was silence for a moment.

'Do you want children?' asked Luke casually.

'Yes. Of course I do. Some day.'

'I thought first-hand experience with Jonty and Matt might have put you off.'

'Absolutely not. I used to love helping with them when they were babies.'

'Some girls might have been embarrassed by their mother's production of twins at the age you were,' he pointed out.

'Were you embarrassed?' she retorted, sitting up.

'No.'

'Then why should I be?'

'All right, put your claws away.' He grinned at her, and smoothed a hand down her cheek, and Saskia gave him an answering grin which turned into a gigantic yawn. Luke set her on her feet and got up.

'Time you were in bed. I assume my normal accommodation is waiting for me?'

'If it wasn't beforehand I'm sure Mother made it so before she went to bed.' Saskia bit her lip. 'I didn't think; I should have offered to do it myself.' She looked up at him, sighing. 'It's your fault.'

'Why mine?' he demanded.

'I was so desperate to be alone with you I forgot about mundane things like clean sheets!'

Luke pulled her into his arms and kissed her at length, to demonstrate his appreciation. It was a long time before he let her go. 'Goodnight, darling. Sleep well.'

'I intend to, if the boys leave me in peace. I was reading to them at three this morning, but they settled down after that so it was worth it.'

'I could do that tonight—'

'Heaven forbid!' She shuddered. 'One look at you and they'd never get to sleep again.'

He laughed, walked with her to the foot of the stairs, set her on the bottom step and kissed her again. 'I'll lock up and see to the lights. Get your head down while you can.'

Saskia jumped out of bed next morning, horrified to see it was past seven. If the twins had woken up in the night she hadn't heard them. She threw on her dressing gown and went along the landing to the boys' room to find them still sleeping, and let out a sigh of relief.

She opened her mother's door gingerly, to find Marina dressing quickly.

'Did they wake up in the night, Mother?' she asked guiltily

'Only once. I gave them drinks, tucked them up, and they went back to sleep.' Marina smiled fondly. 'Don't worry, darling, I'm not about to keel over. Decrepitude hasn't over-taken me quite yet, but I rather fancy some breakfast before the fun starts. Is Luke awake?'

'No idea. I'll throw some clothes on, then I'll be down.'

After orange juice, toast and several cups of coffee, both women felt a great deal better pre-pared to face the day.

'Good heavens,' said Marina, jumping up. 'What a noise up there!'

'The twins have found Luke. You stay there and read the paper,' said Saskia firmly. 'I'll go up and dress them.'

'You spoil me.'

'Only for today. Luke's giving me—and my belongings—a lift back to London tomorrow.'

\*    \*    \*

The day was hectic, but easier on the women with Luke there to help, particularly since his presents for the twins included miniature boxing gloves.

'I thought with these on they couldn't scratch,' said Luke in Saskia's ear.

'If only they don't knock each other out it's a brilliant idea. But it's nearly time for the fish fingers they've demanded for lunch,' she said, 'so use your charm and seniority to get the gloves off now, please. They haven't been eating much lately.'

'Does my charm and seniority work on you, too?' he demanded.

'Every time!'

'I'll remember that.'

After lunch the twins were persuaded to sit still for a while to play the new football board game Luke had brought, and afterwards they watched a Disney video, giving the grown-ups a much-needed breather. But after that the little boys were filled with renewed energy, and it took the combined ingenuity of their mother, Saskia and Luke to keep them amused, since they tended to get fractious now and then as a reminder that they were still far from well.

By late afternoon Marina was exhausted, and Luke and Saskia not much better.

'One game of horses, then upstairs for a bath,' said Luke firmly. 'Mummy's worn out.'

'Me first, me first,' they clamoured, but Saskia solved that problem by volunteering to be one of the mounts.

'Race you to the drawing room and back while Mummy runs your bath,' she said, and got down on her hands and knees with Jonty on her back, while his brother crawled up on Luke. Both of them crowed with glee as Luke and Saskia moved as fast as they could on all fours, with their small jockeys urging them on with much gleeful shouting. Suddenly the front door opened and a burly man with greying tawny hair stood there, laughing.

'I thought you two were supposed to be ill!'

'Daddy! Daddy!' The boys scrambled down to run to their father as their mother came flying downstairs, weariness forgotten.

'Thank God—the cavalry,' said Luke fervently, helping Saskia to her feet.

'Darling!' said Marina, in her husband's embrace. 'You came early!'

'And not a moment too soon, by the look of things.' Professor Armytage looked from his grinning, dishevelled son to his equally untidy, giggling stepdaughter. He kissed Saskia and shook Luke by the hand, his blue eyes bright. 'My thanks to you both. One way and another, I'm very glad to be home.'

# CHAPTER TEN

LUKE and Saskia set off for London through a misty autumn afternoon the following day, well aware that they'd left a very surprised pair of parents behind them.

'Dad's very pleased about the ceasefire,' commented Luke, grinning.

'So's Mother.' Saskia paused. 'Would they be just as pleased if they knew…?'

'Knew what?'

'Exactly what kind of a ceasefire it is.'

'You mean my aim to exchange the role of stepbrother for lover,' he stated baldly.

He threw down the words like a gauntlet, but she made no protest. There was no point in trying to delude herself that she disapproved. She had imagined herself in love with Francis. But that had been self-delusion built on his flattering, all-out pursuit, and the glamour of his lifestyle. And now she felt embarrassed by the memory of it. Because she knew perfectly well that Francis, in common with all other men of her acquaintance, had, at best, served as a substitute for Luke.

Her youthful resentment of Luke's charm and wry good looks would not have survived her adolescence if the ugly duckling had turned into a swan a bit sooner. But by then Luke had taken to avoiding her whenever possible, providing constant fuel for her resentment. Now, at last, she could acknowledge the fact that she had always loved him. That he was the only man in the world she wanted for lover, friend—even father of her children.

The discovery held her rigid in her seat, staring blindly at the crowded road in front of them.

'What is it?' said Luke sharply. 'Do you feel ill?'

'No,' she said with effort. 'Not ill.'

'Then what is it?'

'Nothing. I'm just a bit tired after the exertions of the past couple of days.'

'Hardly surprising. You were brilliant with Jonty and Matt,' he commented. 'Dad was very grateful you went up to lend a hand.'

'In future I'll make a point of going up to Oxford more often.' She flushed. 'I know you do, of course. But in the past I—'

'Kept out of my way,' he said, resigned, and gave her a swift look. 'Do I take it things are different now?'

'Yes. Very different.'

'I'm glad to hear it,' he said with satisfaction. 'By the way, I may know of a job for you. I meant to tell you about it before, but I got sidetracked.'

'Really?' Saskia turned to him eagerly. 'Where? What?'

'During my hunt for furniture I've become quite friendly with a couple who run a large antiques business near my Kensington branch—furniture, porcelain and so on. Their right-hand woman is leaving to have a baby, and they need someone in her place. So far they've had lots of applicants, but no one suitable, so I told them about you.'

'I don't know much about antiques,' said Saskia doubtfully.

'They wouldn't mind that. They're more keen on having someone presentable who fits in. She needs to be computer literate, able to cope with correspondence and accounts, and occasionally even to cope front of shop with clients.' Luke gave her a swift smile. 'I thought all that sounded exactly like you, Sassy. It would mean a drop in salary, of course. They couldn't match your city bank.'

'I'm prepared for that. When could I see them?'

'I made a date provisionally for tomorrow, before you start back to the grind. The other girl won't be leaving for a month, so if it comes off you'd have time to give in your notice.' He glanced at her. 'That's an odd look on your face, Sassy.'

She smiled. 'I was just thinking that a couple of weeks ago I was all set to begin a smart new life with Francis Lawford in his smart riverside apartment, carrying on with my smart city job. And now look at me—contemplating a drop in salary and about to move in with the man most people think of as my brother.'

He reached for her hand. 'It's rather fun to possess our own special secret. Let's keep it that way for the time being, Sassy—give our nearest and dearest time to adjust.'

She slid further down in her seat, her pulse racing at his touch. 'I still can't quite believe it, Lucius Armytage.'

'Neither can I,' he said, and put his hand back on the wheel, breathing in deeply. 'But at the moment it's best I don't even think about it in this blasted traffic. Everyone in Britain seems to be converging on London.'

When they eventually arrived at the house, this time by the more prosaic back entrance, Luke switched on lights in the kitchen, then made several trips out to the car until everything was inside. 'Right, then, Sassy. Let's get this lot upstairs. I haven't changed your bed. I thought you wouldn't mind sleeping in the other stuff since you were only here one night.'

'Not in the least,' she assured him, oddly reassured. If he had plans for rushing her into his own bed they were apparently not to be put into action straight away. She went ahead of him up to the guest room, then exclaimed in surprise at seeing a satinwood wardrobe standing against one wall, looking very much at home with the beautiful bed and the mirror. 'Goodness, how did you manage that?'

'I found it at the Harpers' place when I got back from Italy, which is how I heard about the job. They managed to get it delivered by Friday. Do you like it?'

'It's perfect.' She smiled at him rather awkwardly. 'I'm putting you to a lot of expense.'

He shook his head, grinning. 'Marina, not you. Guests, she informed me, need somewhere to hang their clothes.'

By the time Saskia had unpacked, Luke pronounced himself hungry.

'After all that lunch?' quizzed Saskia, going downstairs.

'I could do with a sandwich, at least. Come down to the kitchen.'

Now that she was actually here, officially committed to living in Luke's house, Saskia was conscious of a faint feeling of constraint.

'What's up?' said Luke quickly as he took food from the box Marina had provided. 'Having second thoughts?'

'No.' She smiled apologetically. 'It's just that I'm not sure how you want things to be between us.'

He looked up with a very direct green gaze. 'I thought I'd made that clear in the car.'

Saskia seized a loaf of bread, and took a knife from the block to hack off a thick, very untidy slice. 'I didn't mean that part of it. What I'm trying to say is that I feel a bit obligated, living here rent-free. Shall I cook for you at night? Or do you eat out? And there's laundry and so on.'

Luke took the knife from her and put a hand either side of her waist to set her on the counter. 'I haven't installed you here as a sort of free domestic help, Sassy. I've been looking after myself for years. Mrs B sees to the chores twice a week, irons my shirts and even does some basic shopping for me. The rest I acquire in whatever type of food emporium I'm nearest when I finish for the day. Does that answer your question?'

'Sort of.'

'It's very simple.' Suddenly he pulled her forward into his arms, and kissed her hard. 'I just want you here with me, Sassy. In my house—and in my bed.'

Taken by surprise, Saskia responded with such fervour that he pulled her closer and kissed her even harder, his breathing suddenly ragged as her mouth and tongue surrendered very explicitly to his. She felt a wave of heat rise in his body, igniting fire in her own. His lips moved hungrily over her face, and he began unbuttoning her shirt, his hands clumsy in his haste instead of the practised speed she would have expected.

Saskia's head went back involuntarily as his mouth found her throat in a series of descending kisses, his fingers caressing her breasts with an urgency she responded to feverishly, her own fingers digging into the muscles of his neck and shoulders. She felt the muscles grow taut beneath her touch, her stomach tensing in response as he fumbled with the buckle of her belt. Then he stopped abruptly, and lifted her down.

'Not here,' Luke said huskily. He took her hand and led her swiftly up the kitchen stairs, then cursed violently as the doorbell rang when they reached the hall.

Saskia dodged into Luke's study as he went to open the door. She rebuckled her belt with trembling fingers and did up her shirt, hoping his visitor would go away quickly—then tensed as an all-too-familiar voice joined with Luke's. Francis! She stared round wildly, like a child looking for a place to hide. Francis, just as she expected, was asking if Luke knew where she was.

'I rang earlier,' she heard him say.

'I've only just come in,' said Luke coolly. 'I haven't checked my messages.'

Saskia's first instinct was to lie low and hope Luke would send Francis away. Then she thought better of it. Time to behave like a responsible adult.

'Hello, Francis,' she said casually, strolling into the hall, where Luke was standing near the door in a way intended to discourage the visitor from any inclination to linger.

Francis was dressed in one of his more casual designer suits, with a silk shirt open at the collar in deference to a non-working day. His dark hair was slightly windblown, but otherwise he looked like an advertisement from a magazine, marred only by the look of incredulity on his spectacularly handsome face.

'*Saskia?*' He started forward, hands outstretched, then stopped in his tracks as Luke moved swiftly to stand by her side. 'Where in hell have you been, Saskia?' Francis demanded angrily. 'I came here tonight as a last resort, just in case Armytage knew where you were.'

'I've been away,' she said evenly.

'I discovered that much from your parents. They refused to tell me where.' His eyes swivelled from her flushed face to Luke's. 'This was the last place I expected to find you.'

'Why?' said Luke.

'Oh, come on, Armytage,' said Francis derisively. 'You know why.'

'You mean because I'm the wicked stepbrother?' Luke exchanged a fleeting smile with Saskia.

Francis ignored him pointedly, and held out a hand to Saskia. 'I think I'm entitled to an explanation. I want a word. Preferably in private.'

'Do *you* want that, Sassy?' enquired Luke.

'Not a lot,' she said frankly. 'But I suppose I owe Francis that much. If you don't mind I'll take him into your study for a few minutes.'

He nodded. 'Right. I'll be close by. Within earshot,' he added.

When he and Saskia were alone in the study Francis closed the door very deliberately. Saskia perched on Luke's desk, her long, denim-clad legs swinging as she smiled at him in polite enquiry. 'So, what did you want to talk about?'

'You know damn well,' he retorted, advancing on her. 'Where the devil did you go? And why? Didn't it occur to you that I might be off my head with worry? What possessed you to vanish like that?'

'I went to Tuscany,' said Saskia, and proceeded to give him, in succinct detail, the reasons for her flight. During the account of her brief visit to his apartment, Francis turned a fiery red.

'It meant nothing!' he broke in. 'I had lunch with Amanda, then we went back to the flat to sign papers, and so on—'

'It was the "so on" I walked in on,' said Saskia caustically.

'It was impulse—an isolated incident. It won't happen again!' he assured her, and reached for her, but she brought up a knee and wreathed her hands around it, effectively discouraging him from getting too close.

'It doesn't matter to me if it does,' she said calmly. 'I admit I was horribly upset at the time, but a large part of that was embarrassment. Rather to my shame I recovered very rapidly. The worst part of it all, in some ways, was having sublet my flat. Luke is putting me up until I find somewhere else.'

Francis began to argue urgently, to persuade her that they could go back to the way things had been, telling her that he loved her, that it was immature to let one isolated incident with Amanda wreck what they had together.

'It's not fair, Saskia. I let you call the tune to show you were something special in my life,' he said with increasing passion. 'You wouldn't go to bed with me until things were settled between us, and I respected that. But, looking back, I'm amazed I was so bloody patient. Is it any wonder I gave in to Amanda that day? If you'd been more amenable in the same department—'

'Ah. So it was my fault! How stupid of me not to realise that.' She eyed him scornfully. 'Come off it, Francis. Be honest. I was there that day. You were in a tearing hurry to get Amanda to bed.'

'So what? That part of our marriage, if nothing else, was always good. It didn't mean anything.' He stared at her uncomprehendingly. 'Are you actually telling me it's over between us due to something stupid like that?'

'Yes,' she said flatly. 'I am. Because it opened my eyes. For me, making love does have to mean something. My little holiday gave me time to think. It finally dawned on me that if I'd really been in love with you I would have wanted to go to bed with you from the first.'

His face took on an ugly look. 'You hellish little teaser!' He moved towards her with menace. 'I've a good mind—'

'No, you don't,' growled Luke from the doorway, and Francis backed away, scowling.

Luke lifted Saskia from the desk and put an arm round her. 'Are you all right?'

She smiled up at him in reassurance. 'Fine. Francis was just leaving.'

Francis, however, when they eventually had attention to spare for him, was watching them with dawning comprehension. 'So that's it!' he sneered, and eyed Saskia in furious disgust. 'You had the nerve to sermonise to me for making love with my ex-wife, when all the time your filthy little game was *incest*?'

Whereupon Luke's fist connected with Francis's angry face, and sent him sprawling through the doorway into the hall, flat on his back.

'I'll have you for that, Armytage,' Francis howled as he scrambled to his feet.

'Come on, then,' invited Luke, advancing on him. 'No time like the present.'

Francis gave him a glare of pure malevolence. 'I meant the law, Armytage. I'll prosecute. Better still I'll cancel your contract with my restaurants.'

'You mean your father's restaurants,' corrected Luke, opening the door. 'Get out,

Lawford. Otherwise *I*'ll bring in the law, and
have you up for trespass.'

Francis brushed past him, then turned in the
doorway, smoothing back his hair as he eyed
Saskia in appeal. 'You really mean to stay
here—with him?'

'For the time being, yes. I should get something to put on that eye,' she added kindly. 'Ice
at the very least.'

Luke shut the door on their visitor's incensed, rapidly discolouring face, and took
Saskia in his arms. 'Are you all right?'

'Yes,' she said, muffled against his shirt-
front. Then she looked up at him with sudden
anxiety. 'But Francis was a good customer.
Will it affect you very much if he does with-
draw his order?'

'Not enough to put me out of business,' he
assured her.

'But it was a big order. I should know; he
told me often enough! And you've just bought
this place, and you haven't furnished it properly yet. Let me ask Francis to reconsider—'
She halted at the look in his eyes. 'What's so
funny?'

'I wouldn't describe it as "funny" exactly,' he said, taking her by the hand. 'Do you honestly think Francis would listen to you, under the circumstances?'

'I suppose not—where are you taking me?'

'To bed.'

They were halfway up the stairs when the phone rang. Luke threw up his hands in despair. 'Is there a conspiracy against us?'

He raced with her up to the bedroom and picked up the telephone alongside his bed, pulling Saskia down to lie beside him. 'Oh, sorry, Marina. We were late getting in, then Saskia's ex-friend Lawford called round—no, no, she's fine. I'll call her.' He held the phone away for a moment, his hand over the receiver, grinning down into Saskia's scarlet face, then passed it over to her for a chat—which became increasingly difficult as Luke began unbuttoning her shirt while she was trying to talk.

'Are you all right, darling?' said Marina anxiously. 'You sound a bit strange. Was Francis nasty?'

'A bit,' said Saskia in a constricted tone, trying to halt Luke's hands. 'But nothing I couldn't handle. How are the twins?'

Marina went on to give a reassuring report on their progress, asked again if Saskia was feeling well, and only put an end to the conversation when her daughter promised to ring again next day to confirm that she wasn't coming down with something.

'You monster!' she panted as Luke put the phone back. 'How did you expect me to carry on a conversation when you were—?'

'Doing this?' he said huskily, and proceeded, in a very leisurely and relishing way, to undress her. 'I've been wanting to from the moment I found you in the bath, Saskia Ford. If you stop me now I'm likely to explode into a thousand pieces.'

'Then I won't,' she whispered, but put a hand over her eyes as Luke finished his task with tormenting slowness. Afterwards he lay propped on one elbow, his eyes moving over her in relishing silence.

'What a lot of time we've wasted,' he said, in a voice rendered hoarse by desire. 'I want you so much, Sassy.'

Her eyes flew open at that, the words reaching something deep inside that settled and warmed her as though the last of her doubts had been laid to rest.

'Have you any idea how hard it was to leave you alone with Lawford just now?' he demanded. 'I wanted to do a whole lot more than black his eye.' Luke stood up, and with sudden impatience stripped off his clothes, then lay down beside her and took her into his arms, one long-fingered hand moulding her against him from head to toe.

He made no comment on the fact that she was shaking like a jelly, noted Saskia, deeply touched because Luke was merely holding her close and making no attempt to begin the hasty onslaught which had been her experience in the past.

'Relax,' he said in her ear, his breath hot against her skin. 'We've got all night. Because if anyone else rings up, or hammers on my door, they're out of luck.' He drew her closer. 'Stop trembling, Sassy. Delectable though you may be, I'm not going to eat you.'

As a lover's opening gambit it was remarkably successful. Saskia not only relaxed, she thrust herself closer, and evoked an anguished groan for her pains.

'I'm trying to take this slowly,' and Luke severely, and put her away. 'Just lie there so I can look at you.'

'But that's not fair,' she objected, turning her head away.

'All's fair in love, Sassy.' He brought her face back to his, smiling in a way which roused a fiery response in every secret, melting part of her. With slow, savouring pleasure he began to kiss and caress her inch by inch, leaving no part of her body neglected. At first she did her best to lie still, but her breath grew laboured, her pulse raced, her head tossed back and forth on the pillow, and at last her exploring fingers dug into his shoulders in such frantic demand that his mouth closed on hers, and he grasped her hips, lifting them to his, so that their bodies fitted together with all the miraculous exactitude of two halves becoming whole.

Saskia gasped, her mouth open against his, as he began to move gently, subtly at first, until his own need overtook him and he made love to her with a frenzy she urged him to with arts she'd never realised she possessed. At last she stiffened, cried out, and Luke held her close as they gasped together in the culmination he had taken such great care to ensure she experienced before he did.

It was a long time before Luke moved, and when he did it was only to draw the covers over them and hold the sleeping girl more comfortably in his arms. When Saskia woke, an hour or so later, she looked up into Luke's face with a smile of such triumph he laughed, and rubbed his nose against hers. 'You see?' he said lazily.

She ran the tip of her tongue over her lips. 'See what?' she said cautiously.

'It isn't mandatory to separate after making love.'

Heat rose in her cheeks. 'No,' she agreed, and stretched luxuriously all along the hard length of him. 'I'm just sorry I wasted so much time before I found out,' she said with regret.

He shook his head in wonder. 'Hard to believe, now, that only a short time ago you were as friendly as a caged tigress towards me, and that I really did think of you as a younger sister.'

Saskia gazed at him thoughtfully. 'And was it really just one look that changed all that, when you found me at the villa?'

Luke traced a finger down her cheek. 'It certainly opened my eyes to the fact that you'd grown up into a very desirable woman. And gradually, as I spent more time in your company in the days that followed, it became clearer by the minute that my feelings towards you weren't fraternal in the slightest. And then, the night of the Harleys' *vendemmia* party, watching you dance with Dante and the others, I felt so damn jealous I had to hold back from snatching you away. It was becoming a matter of urgency to stop you thinking of me as a brother.'

'But that was my particular problem from the moment you arrived in my life—I never did think of you as a brother,' she confessed. 'I used my hostility as a smokescreen to hide my real feelings towards you. Even from myself.'

'So how do you feel now?'

'Utterly wonderful.' She smiled at him, her eyes glittering. 'Also hungry. Didn't you say something earlier about sandwiches?'

# CHAPTER ELEVEN

NEXT morning, after Luke had left for the day, Saskia went off to the interview at the large, elegant Kensington shop where Theo and Margaret Harper sold porcelain and antique furniture. They were a very friendly couple, and after a quick look at Saskia's CV they gave her a tour of the premises, introduced her to the existing staff, then took her up to their flat for coffee.

'I don't mind telling you,' said Margaret, who was an elegant blonde woman in her forties, 'that the people we've interviewed so far just wouldn't have fitted in. We need to have confidence in our employees, since we spend so much time at auctions and house sales and so on.' She exchanged a look with her husband, then smiled at Saskia. 'We both feel that you'd be an asset to our team, Miss Ford. So instead of beating about the bush we may as well tell you that the job's yours if you want it.'

Saskia went off to ring her mother with the glad news, then headed for the pub Luke frequented for lunch. She sat down at a secluded table at the back of the bar, feeling very pleased with herself and life in general as she ordered a glass of mineral water.

The place was full by the time Luke came hurrying in. His face lit up as he spotted her, and she got up, giving him a thumbs-up sign of triumph as he weaved his way through the tables towards her.

'You got the job!' He gave her a swift, jubilant kiss, then moved his chair closer and demanded all the details of her interview. 'I knew the Harpers would like you,' he said, when she'd finished.

'Why?'

'How could they help it?' he said simply. 'By the way', he said, after they'd ordered lunch. 'I had a phone call from young Dante this morning. He's coming over today and wants to know if he can take you out to dinner.'

Saskia's eyes widened. 'What did you say?'

Luke gave her an evil grin. 'I told him to ring you later at the house and ask you himself.'

'You did *what*?' she demanded wrathfully.

He shrugged, the grin widening. 'You're usually banging on about independence and equality and so on. I didn't dare answer for you.'

'Just for that, Lucius Armytage, I shall accept his invitation with pleasure,' she retorted.

'By all means,' he said, with deflating promptness. 'But only if I come, too.'

They exchanged a long look, full of mutual memories of the night before. Her lips parted, and Luke leaned nearer involuntarily, then the waitress interrupted them with two plates of food neither of them did much justice to.

'See what you reduce me to?' said Luke, eyeing his bowl of mussels without enthusiasm. 'I've lost my appetite.'

'I'll come off my equality soap-box and make dinner for you tonight,' she promised. 'I'm not hungry either.'

'Don't wear yourself out,' said Luke, eyes gleaming. 'I'd rather you ordered dinner in than get too tired.'

'I shall cook,' she said firmly. 'I've lost you a very remunerative order, remember? So I'm not going to waste money on takeaway food when I can whip something up for a lot less.'

'A pearl above price,' he murmured, stroking the back of her hand. 'However, if you're talking about Francis, have no fear. Lawford Senior sent me a fax doubling the order for the French house wine I supplied last month. It's going down very well indeed, he informed me. The heir apparent will have his work cut out to cancel something that's making the restaurants a substantial profit.'

'Oh, dear,' said Saskia, shaking her head. 'Francis isn't going to like that. I remember he was a bit caustic over that feature on you in the press when your book was published—not to mention the flattering photograph.'

'I didn't know you'd seen that,' said Luke, moving closer.

'Mother showed it to me.'

'Joel Gilbert did the piece, actually. The man you met at the party. Joel did a piece on Francis, too, a while back.'

'Really? I didn't know that was Joel's work.' Saskia chuckled. 'Francis was a bit miffed because the piece was very brief and didn't include the photograph he supplied.'

'Forget Francis,' said Luke dismissively, his hand tightening on hers. 'I'll try to get home earlier tonight.'

'Don't think I'm going to cook for you every night,' she informed him, her eyes belying the tartness in her voice. 'Once I'm back at the bank you'll be lucky to get a sandwich.'

'A dinner of herbs will do equally well,' he assured her, and shot to his feet as he looked at the clock. 'Is that the time? I must go. I've got some shipments arriving at the warehouse this afternoon, which will please my mail-order staff.'

Outside, Luke kissed her quickly, then hailed a taxi and put her in it. 'See you later, Sassy. Be good.'

Saskia had been honest about her eating habits after a day at the bank. On evenings in, alone at the flat, she ate salad or took something home from a delicatessen. And Francis had preferred restaurants to home-cooked suppers.

But tonight, Saskia decided, as the taxi set her down at the supermarket nearest Luke's house, she would pull out all the stops.

She was in the kitchen, stirring something in a pan, when he came through the door, his eyes alight with pleasure at the sight of her in a striped butcher's apron protecting the clinging brown dress. She laid down her wooden spoon and held her face up for his kiss as though this were something they'd been doing for years.

'You've got half an hour,' she warned when he let her go.

He sprang to attention smartly. 'Yes, ma'am! Do I get a prize if I'm early?'

She gave him a prim smile. 'Possibly.'

Luke made for the stairs, then turned to look at her. 'I like this, Sassy. I like it a lot.'

She nodded gravely. 'So do I.'

Both pairs of green eyes met in perfect accord, then he smiled his lopsided smile and took the stairs two at a time, all sign of weariness vanished.

When Luke returned, his long legs encased in silvery-drab needlecord, he was wearing a green silk shirt the colour of his eyes.

'We're having fish,' said Saskia, controlling her pleasure at the sight of him. 'So I leave the choice of wine to you.'

Luke kissed her nose as he passed her on the way to the refrigerator in the pantry. He came back with a very impressive bottle of champagne in his hand. 'I've had this waiting since your promise to come and live with me.'

'I thought I was only agreeing to a rent-free room, Lucius Armytage,' she reminded him, then smiled to take the sting out of the words. 'All the rest came as a wonderful bonus.'

He bowed gracefully. 'Which we shall celebrate, whatever we're eating, with this venerable Krug.'

Saskia watched, impressed, as he eased out the champagne cork. 'No showerbath?' she commented.

'Just a wisp of smoke like the sigh of a satisfied woman,' he informed her, lips twitching.

'You'd know more than me about that!' she retorted as he went over to a cupboard to search for some flutes.

'Are you paying me a compliment?' he asked, chuckling, as he handed her a glass of champagne.

'I suppose I am,' she admitted, flushing. 'So, what shall we drink to?'

'To our ceasefire,' he said promptly. 'May it never be broken.'

'Amen to that,' she agreed, and took a mouthful of wine. 'Oh, Luke, this is glorious. Even to my uneducated palate.'

They sat nibbling nuts and sipping the champagne, talking non-stop about Luke's day and the prospect of Saskia's new job.

'Dante rang, by the way,' she said at one point. 'He laughed when I said you insisted on coming to dinner, too. He's got such good manners—insisted he's delighted.'

'He's also too good-looking by far, and if you think I'm letting you out alone with him you're mistaken.'

'I do love it when you're masterful,' she teased, then eyed the shirt. 'That matches your eyes. Did you buy it for the precise purpose of seducing your dinner partners?'

'Certainly not.' Luke smiled virtuously. 'It was a present.'

Saskia sniffed. 'Zoë, I suppose?'

'Actually, no. It was your mother.' He smiled smugly. 'Did I make you jealous?'

'Was that your intention?'

'Absolutely.'

'In your dreams,' she retorted, eyes flashing, then jumped to her feet as the oven-timer went off. She went over and removed a baking dish which held a foil parcel. She slit it open, then brought the dish over for him to inspect.

Luke eyed the magnificent fillet of fish smothered in herbs, then smiled up at her. 'Ah. ''Better is a dinner of herbs where love is,''' he quoted.

'Otherwise known as my Italian grandmother's way with sea-bass,' said Saskia, pleased he'd got the point.

'You,' said Luke, after an interval of serious eating, 'are the most amazing cook, Sassy. I'm impressed.'

'I do the same as you,' she informed him, mouth full. 'I only attempt the things within my capabilities. Which means you had a salad with the fish, and for pudding apple pie from the local bakery. But as a consolation I've made proper custard—a fairly new talent I learned at home recently, because Jonty and Matt adore the stuff.'

'If it's Marina's recipe I'm a happy man. Very happy,' said Luke, putting down his knife and fork with a sigh. He refilled her glass with champagne. 'Have some of this while we bid farewell to that magnificent fish.'

Saskia sipped with caution. 'This is my second glass, so I'll go slowly.' She grinned. 'Otherwise you may have to put me to bed again.'

'Since I'm going to do that anyway, why not risk a taste more Krug?' He let out a deep breath in response to the glittering look she gave him. 'Though if you eye me in that precise way, Sassy, you risk being put to bed right now.'

She shook her head. 'Not,' she said firmly, 'until we've eaten the pudding.'

* * *

Saskia found it very hard to detach herself from Luke's arms next morning and get ready for her first day back at the bank. Not only because she had no wish to get out of bed, but because Luke objected strongly to letting her go.

'What time will you be home?' he demanded, hands behind his head as he watched her wrap herself in her dressing gown.

'Haven't a clue,' she said gloomily. 'Knowing my dear boss, he'll have a pile of leftover work for me before I even get to grips with the current stuff. While you're enjoying yourself with your vintage nectar think of me among the financial warfare.'

'I will think of you. And of this, Sassy. Far more than I should.' His eyes held hers, and without a word she melted into his outstretched arms.

In consequence, although she skipped breakfast and Luke drove her to the underground, Saskia arrived on the trading floor of the bank fifteen minutes late, to find Charles Harrison waiting for her with a face like thunder.

But it would have taken more than Charles Harrison's wrath to chasten her on this particular morning, thought Saskia, when she finally got to grips with her workload. There were several messages from the switchboard on her desk, reporting calls from Francis Lawford during her absence, and she tore them up with much satisfaction, then plunged into the usual chaotic demands of the day.

Instead of going out to lunch, Saskia sent out for a sandwich and ate it at her desk while she composed her letter of resignation. Afterwards she went straight on with her work, eager to leave near her usual time, only to be interrupted by Charles brandishing her resignation in fury. She sat, unmoved, while he raged and stormed at her, until at last he changed tactics and offered a substantial rise in salary. She refused it politely, assured him she was not getting married, and reminded him to leave promptly since Mrs Harrison had guests for dinner.

Saskia was very tired when she left the bank a good half-hour later than intended. She emerged into pouring rain, and to her intense dismay found Francis waiting outside under an umbrella.

'I need a word,' he said, seizing her arm.

'Well, I don't,' she retorted angrily, trying to free herself.

'I strongly advise you to listen.'

Something vicious in his tone alarmed her. 'Why?'

'I've got the car parked on a meter round the corner. I'll drive you home.'

'No, thanks. To the nearest underground will do.'

He shrugged, keeping her arm in a vice-like grip until they reached his Jaguar. Inside, he turned to her urgently, his features sharpened by the street light shining into the car. 'Is this really what you want?' he demanded.

'What do you mean?'

'You know bloody well what I mean!' He thrust his face forward so she could see his bruised eye. 'I mean your incestuous relationship with the lout who gave me this.'

'You know perfectly well that Luke and I are not related, Francis,' she said irritably.

'Oh, yes, *I* know.' He sat back in his seat, the satisfaction plain to see on his bruised face. 'But others don't. Soon it will be common knowledge that Lucius bloody Armytage is having fun and games with his sister. I've got a contact who works on the evening paper all our friends read—the one who did such a flattering little feature on the young wine entrepreneur and his new book. After all, darling, the resemblance between the two of you may be coincidental, but it's very convincing. Once a photograph of you appears alongside Luke's all the world and his wife will believe it whether it's true or not. Incest has such a sexy ring to it. But it won't do much for Armytage's business.'

Saskia stared at him, feeling sick, as her mind grappled with the connotations. Joel Gilbert, of course, was the journalist friend. And she'd been introduced to him as Luke's little sister at the Harleys' party. Luke could sue, of course, if the titbit was published. But some mud always sticks. And with a shudder she pictured the effect on her mother and Sam.

'I must have been mad,' she said slowly at last as she stared at Francis.

'To move in with Armytage?' he demanded eagerly.

'No. To have ever imagined I could share my life with you.'

'But I *love* you, Saskia,' he said in desperation. 'I'll even marry you—'

'Not on your life,' she said swiftly, then breathed in deeply as inspiration struck. 'In any case, you can't. Because I'm going to marry Luke. I'm sure you'll appreciate being the first to know—Luke and I are engaged.'

Francis, who was no fool, stared at her in furious comprehension.

She nodded kindly. 'That's right, Francis. It rather shoots your story down, doesn't it? So you'd better get onto your tame hack and say your scoop's no-go. Not, for a moment, that I think he would have had it published. The lawyers at the paper in question are surely too clever for that?'

'They might have done,' he said bitterly, 'if the wording had been euphemistic enough. Or if he'd sold it to a less fussy tabloid. All right, you little witch. You win.'

'Thank you, Francis. I was sure you'd see sense. Goodbye,' she added absently, her eyes on an approaching taxi, and before he could say a word she'd dived out of the car to flag it down.

Luke had left a message on his answer machine to say he wouldn't be home until late, due to an unexpected dinner with a valued client. He told her to eat a proper meal and go to bed early if she was tired. 'I'll come and tuck you in,' he added in a different tone, just as the message ended.

Saskia was both disappointed and relieved. She needed time before talking to Luke. The encounter with Francis had left her feeling grubby, and in desperate need of the kind of bath she'd been used to when living on her own.

Afterwards, after a lonely, perfunctory supper off a tray, she found she couldn't quite bring herself to get into Luke's bed on her own. A bit late in the day to be shy, she told herself irritably, but in the end she climbed into the brass bed in the guest room and turned her radio on low. Worn out by the various events of the day, she fell asleep almost at once, deaf to the disc jockey's muted pleasantries, and never saw the tall figure who came in silently and turned the radio off, then switched off her light.

'I'm sorry I didn't wait up for you,' she said in remorse as, fully dressed and ready for the day next morning, she came out onto the landing to see Luke leaning in his doorway in his dressing gown, looking as haggard as she felt. 'It was a hectic day.'

'My problem was a hectic night,' he said bitterly, with a hand to his head.

'Too much of the Sangiovese grape?' she asked in sympathy, reaching up to kiss him.

'And every other kind,' he sighed, holding her close. 'It's hard to refuse when the other man's paying and also happens to be one of my best customers.' Luke tried to smile, but gave up. 'Can't do that. It hurts.' He looked at his watch. 'You're earlier this morning.'

'I had more sleep last night.' She bit her lip at the gleam in his bloodshot eyes and started downstairs. 'I'll make you some tea.'

Since Luke was obviously in no state to hear about her run-in with Francis, Saskia decided to leave it until the evening to give details. It was only when she was emerging from the underground to make for the bank that she remembered they were dining out with Dante, and sighed morosely. Dante was a very charming young man, but tonight, after the inevitable hassle of her day, she would have much preferred a quiet evening with Luke and an early night. Also with Luke.

Despite all her efforts, it was late when she got home that evening, to find that both Dante and another unexpected visitor were already in the study with Luke.

'Hello, darling,' said Luke, coming to greet her, a very odd glitter in his eyes as he took her in his arms and kissed her very deliberately on the mouth.

'Hi,' said Saskia, taken aback, then went forward to take Dante's hand.

'*Buona sera*, Saskia,' he said, kissing her hand with grace. He straightened, smiling. 'As you see, I am early, and there is another visitor here also.'

Saskia smiled brightly at the small, exquisitely dressed girl. 'Why, Zoë. How nice to see you,' she lied.

'Hello, Saskia.' Zoë gave her a cool little smile. 'I was in the neighbourhood, so I thought I'd drop by and offer my congratulations.'

Luke put an arm round Saskia's waist, squeezing it significantly as his eyes speared hers. 'Zoë read something in the paper tonight—about our rumoured engagement.'

'It is a great sorrow for me to hear it,' said Dante, smiling at a dumbstruck Saskia. 'You told me you were Luke's *sorellastra*, but I did not realise you were not related at all.'

'Neither did I,' said Zoë sweetly.

'But you spent Christmas Day with the family in Oxford last year,' said Saskia. 'I thought you knew.'

'You were always so offhand with me she took it for granted you really were a sister of some kind,' said Luke, with an edge to his voice. He tightened his arm, smiling down at her. 'Now, of course, everything's different.'

'Obviously,' said Zoë, and cast an eye at Dante. 'So, how do you fit into the picture, Mr Fortinari?'

'Call me Dante, please.' He smiled at her. 'My family knows Luke well. He does business with us. I met Saskia when she and Luke were staying at the Villa Rosa near my home recently.'

Zoë's eyes narrowed. 'Ah. The Tuscany Fortinaris. I thought the name was familiar. Luke must have mentioned it. He likes talking about his work.'

Saskia, who was eight inches taller and several pounds heavier than the unfailingly elegant Zoë, felt very untidy and unappealing after her exhausting day, and fervently hoped the girl would leave soon so she could have a bath.

But instead of getting up to go, Zoë handed her a copy of the evening paper, folded at the relevant section. 'Have you seen this yet?'

Saskia shook her head. Her eyes widened as she saw a blurred picture of Luke kissing her in the pub, and read that Luke Armytage—the young wine entrepreneur who had featured recently in the features section—was rumoured to be engaged to the beautiful Saskia Ford, daughter of the lady his father, Professor Samuel Armytage, had married ten years previously.

'Dear me,' she said at last. 'I wonder how that got in there?'

'I was wondering that, too,' said Luke casually. 'But, since the secret's out, let's celebrate. Perhaps you'd like to join us for dinner, Zoë?'

Both Dante and Zoë were so delighted by the invitation Saskia had no option. She smiled brightly and excused herself to get ready.

Later, hair gleaming, face painted with rather more emphasis than usual, Saskia rejoined the others, wearing a scarlet jacket over a brief black shift dress, the gold hoops in her ears swinging against her rapidly lengthening hair—every detail calculated to contrast with Zoë's pastel-pink suit.

'*Bellissima!*' applauded Dante.

'Amazing,' agreed Luke, something in his voice raising the hairs on Saskia's neck.

The evening, on the surface, was a success. They dined in a north London restaurant famed for the numbers of writers, film makers and television producers among its clientele. The food was both good and unpretentious, the wine came up to both men's high standards, and Zoë, who knew several of the recognisable diners well enough to wave at, scintillated accordingly. Dante was charmed with everything, Saskia with nothing. She was so conscious of the smouldering beneath Luke's *bonhomie* that the food on her plate could have been sawdust for all the pleasure she took in it.

Matters grew worse when both Dante and Zoë insisted on discussing the engagement, teasing them about wedding bells.

'We haven't done much thinking on the subject yet,' said Luke lazily, smiling at Saskia.

'No,' she agreed. They hadn't done much thinking about anything other than the pressing need to share a bed—something she rather fancied Luke was regretting as of now. Rumours of an engagement, exaggerated or not, were quite obviously not to his taste.

The evening ended at last when Dante took Zoë home in one taxi while Saskia and Luke took another back to the house. The journey was accomplished in total silence which had stretched Saskia's nerves to breaking point by the time Luke unlocked his handsome front door. She went ahead of him into the hall and stood irresolute, wondering what to do next.

'Perhaps,' said Luke, very quietly, 'we could have a little chat before you go up to bed.'

*You* go up to bed, not *we*, thought Saskia miserably. Not that she felt in the least like escaping to any bed except her own at this precise juncture. And even that bed belonged to Luke.

'Of course.' She took off her jacket and hung it on the newel post, then went through the study door he was holding open for her. She sat down in a corner of the sofa, crossing her long legs in the sheer black stockings that were her weakness.

Luke half sat on the desk, one foot swinging back and forth like a pendulum. 'I think before we start I'd like to make one or two things clear.'

She said nothing and sat composedly, waiting for him to rid himself of the burden he'd been carrying all evening.

'I'm a pretty old-fashioned, conventional sort of guy at heart,' he began conversationally. 'I always assumed that when the time came I would be the one to do the proposing. Who did you talk to, Saskia, to get that piece in the paper? Was it Joel? He was sniffing round you enough at the Harleys' party.'

'You think *I* was responsible?' Saskia demanded, eyes glittering icily. 'Why on earth would I do such a stupid thing?'

'To force my hand, maybe.' Luke stared down at his swinging foot.

'Force your hand?' she repeated blankly, then her eyes flashed sudden green fire. 'You mean stampede you to the altar?' Saskia jumped to her feet. 'Thanks a lot!' She turned to make for the door, but Luke shot upright and caught her wrist, jerking her round to face him.

'Who else could have done it?'

'Why not try whoever it was who took the photograph?' she said through her teeth. 'Let me go. You're hurting me.'

Luke dropped her hand, but stood with his back to the door, barring her way. 'You must have some idea of how it happened. I don't. So who else knows—or is even interested in— the fact that you and I share a house now?'

She looked at him for a long, tense interval, then shrugged and turned away. 'All right, you may as well know the truth.'

# CHAPTER TWELVE

'ARE you saying you *were* responsible?' Luke demanded, his face draining of colour, demonstrating all too clearly he'd hoped Saskia wasn't the culprit. 'Couldn't you have let nature take its course, Saskia? I strongly object to having my hand forced. Even by you.' He closed his eyes for a moment. 'Especially by you,' he added, as though the words choked him.

Saskia's chin lifted proudly. 'I wasn't forcing your hand. It was more a damage limitation exercise. Francis met me outside the bank last night, and told me he'd sent a juicy little piece, via his journalist friend, to the paper who did the feature on you—thought it would be a nice little follow-up for readers to learn that the young wine entrepreneur was involved in a questionable relationship with his sister. Francis said everyone would remark on this inconvenient resemblance of ours in the photograph that went with it. I didn't realise the shot was such a recent one.'

'Plenty of photographers and journalists frequent the Royal Oak.' Luke's shoulders came away from the door. 'But they couldn't have published it, Saskia. It's libel.'

'I told Francis that,' she agreed. 'But he assured me that if it was euphemistic enough something could be made out of it. And, human nature being what it is, some mud invariably sticks whether it's the truth or not. So I was struck by this utterly brilliant idea, and sabotaged his little scheme by saying we were engaged.' She gave him a disdainful smile. 'I never thought for a moment that the news would be of interest to anyone but Francis. The other slant would have been, of course. But to be honest, Luke, I was thinking of our respective parents as much as you. I just couldn't take the risk.'

Luke stared down at her, his face like a mask. 'I apologise,' he said stiffly. 'I should have known—'

'If Dante and Zoë hadn't been here I would have told you as soon as I came in tonight.'

She shrugged. 'Anyway, all is now explained. Francis would be pleased if he knew.'

'Knew what?'

'That he's had his revenge for his black eye.'

'He's lucky his injury wasn't worse,' retorted Luke grimly.

'Lucky for us all,' she agreed lightly. 'Otherwise who knows what havoc he might have created? Goodnight, Luke.'

He stayed where he was, barring her exit. 'Where are you going?'

She stared at him. 'To bed. Where else?'

'You haven't given me time to apologise properly—' he began, but she held up a peremptory hand.

'Please don't bother.' She raked a weary hand through her hair. 'Let me pass, Luke. I'm very tired.'

'I hope you resigned from that blasted job,' he said sharply.

'Oh, yes. I burnt my boats right on schedule.' She managed a smile. 'My boss was not pleased. Mainly because he's unlikely to find anyone else likely to put up with him the way I do.'

'I can well believe that.' Luke rubbed a hand over his eyes and stood aside. 'All right, then, Saskia. I'll let you get off to bed. Perhaps we can talk things over more amicably tomorrow evening, when we've both calmed down.'

'Perhaps.'

Luke caught her by the shoulders and bent his head to kiss her, but Saskia moved her face away and he released her instantly, his face grim. 'It was only a goodnight kiss, not a request to share my bed.'

She nodded matter-of-factly. 'I'm aware of that. But oddly enough, Luke, I don't feel very cordial towards you right now. And just before we lay the subject to rest I'd like it understood that the thought of marrying you never entered my head. Until very recently I looked on our relationship in a vastly different light.'

'You adjusted to the change very well. Or have you forgotten our nights together already?' he pointed out, his eyes glittering like a tiger's.

'Of course I haven't. You're a very accomplished lover, as well you know,' she said sweetly. 'But it was never intended as a permanent arrangement, Luke, and please don't try to kid me that you thought otherwise. Your objection to the news item proved that.' She yawned suddenly, more from nerves than weariness. 'Anyway, there's no point in going over the same ground. My intentions were the best, but it all went wrong somewhere. I—I'm sorry,' she added, her voice thickening. 'Goodnight.'

Somewhere around six next morning Saskia gave up all pretence of trying to sleep. Without turning on a light, she crept downstairs to the kitchen with the suitcases she'd packed the night before and went out into the cold morning to make for the underground. Her early arrival caused no comment at the bank, where the trading floor at the bank was in full swing, as usual, by seven-thirty. Saskia dumped her luggage in the cloakroom, then rang her tenant, Carol Parker, who had a job similar to her own in a rival bank.

When Saskia asked if she could beg a bed on her own sitting-room sofa for a day or two Carol consented readily, expressing surprise that Saskia was not, after all, living in luxurious sin in Docklands with Francis Lawford. Saskia thanked Carol gratefully, confirmed she still had a key, then put the phone down to greet Charles Harrison, who was brandishing the previous day's evening paper.

'I thought you weren't getting married,' he thundered.

'I'm not, Mr Harrison. It's a mistake.'

Saskia let herself into the familiar Chiswick flat that night to find a note on the counter in the minuscule kitchen informing her that Carol was at a party and wouldn't be home that night, and if anything appealed to Saskia in the food line she was to help herself.

It was only then that Saskia rang her mother to chat for a while and ask about Sam and the twins, and then, as if it were an afterthought, she mentioned her move, and explained that sharing with Luke hadn't been a good idea after all.

'Why ever not?' demanded Marina in con-
sternation.

'The same old reasons, Mother. Neither
leopard had changed its spots.'

'But you seemed to be getting on so well
when the boys were ill.'

'We were. But it didn't last. Don't worry.
No bones broken, or blood spilt.' She paused.
'If Luke should ask you where I am, just tell
him I've found somewhere else and don't have
a phone yet.'

'Nor an address?' said Marina tartly.

'Look, Mother, we had a row. Nothing
dreadful, but for the time being I'd very much
like to keep out of Luke's way for a bit.'

'Do you expect me to lie?'

'No. Just tell him I'd rather not talk to him.'

'And I'd rather you told him yourself, my
girl.' Marina sighed. 'Oh, very well. But I
don't like it.'

Neither did she, thought Saskia drearily, and
took some clothes from her luggage in readi-
ness for the next day.

Half an hour later her mother rang back.

'Luke rang, right on cue,' she said unhappily. 'Apparently he was late home tonight and had only just discovered you'd moved out.'

'What did he say?'

'Nothing much. But he seemed very upset.'

'Did he ask for my phone number?'

'Yes. I told him you refused to let me pass it on. I didn't enjoy that.'

'Ah, but you adore Luke, Mother.'

'True. Not as much as I do you, Saskia, but I am fond of him,' said Marina with dignity. 'Now, try to get some sleep. And come down on Saturday morning for the weekend, please.'

Since this was more by nature of an order than a request, Saskia didn't dare refuse. Not that she wanted a weekend in town on her own, she thought, sighing, and looked round her at the familiar surroundings.

Only a short time ago this had been home to her. But not any more. Her short sojourn in Luke's lovely old house had seen to that. Already she was beginning to regret her hasty, headlong flight from it. And from Luke. But his reaction to the news item had hurt. At the thought, her anger came flooding back in full force. Her aim had been to prevent harm to him and his business, while he had jumped to the usual male conclusion that she was pushing him into holy matrimony. And an unholy affair it would have been with a start like that, she thought scornfully.

Next day work went hard. Two sleepless nights in a row were no help with her job, which was stressful at the best of times. By the evening she was heartily sick of trading figures and computer screens, and wanted nothing more than a hot bath and an early night. Which was unlikely, since she would have to banish Carol from the sitting room to achieve it.

When Saskia was making for the underground, among a crowd of other city workers, she felt a hand on her arm and turned to see Luke, dressed in the raincoat that made him look even taller and more formidable than usual.

'Saskia,' he said peremptorily. 'I want to talk to you.'

For a moment she was so delighted by the sight of him she was ready to agree to anything he wanted. But pride came to her rescue. 'I'm tired and I want to get—' She halted, and he smiled grimly.

'Where, Saskia? Where did you run to this time? You needn't worry,' he added. 'I shan't add trespass to my sins. But I would like to know you're safe somewhere.'

They stood in the middle of the pavement with home-going commuters rushing past, jostling them, making conversation impossible.

'All right,' she said will ill grace. 'Did you come by car?'

He nodded. 'It's parked round the corner. I was lucky. Someone drove off as I arrived.'

'I'm back in my old flat in Chiswick for a day or two,' she said, falling into step with him. 'Thank you for the lift. I'm a bit tired.'

Once they were on their way in the car he glanced at her pale face, which was drained still further by the street lights.

'"A bit tired" is something of an understatement,' he commented. 'You look exhausted, Saskia.'

No more 'Sassy', she thought forlornly. 'It's hectic at the bank. And my boss isn't in a very sweet mood since I gave in my notice. I'm only required to work to the end of the calendar month, by the way, so I can start the new job in two weeks' time, which will give me a few days first to find somewhere to live. Preferably near Harper's.'

'You already have a place to live near Harper's. Why the devil did you take off like that?' he demanded bitterly.

'You know perfectly well!' she snapped. 'It all went wrong. If I'd stayed I'd have been guarding every word in case you suspected my intentions.' She snorted inelegantly. 'It's utterly ludicrous. Believe me, Lucius Armytage, if I really wanted to marry you I'd use subtler means than an item in the press to persuade you.'

'What would you do?' he asked instantly.

'No idea!' She eyed him balefully. 'Marriage isn't on my personal agenda. But if it were I'd think up something cleverer than that!'

There was silence for a moment as Luke negotiated a particularly busy roundabout. Then he said abruptly, 'When we get to your flat I want to come up for a moment. It's impossible to talk in the car.'

'Carol may be there.'

'Then if she is I shall say goodnight very politely and leave you in peace. For tonight, anyway.'

Saskia shrugged. 'Very well. If you must.'

The rest of the journey was accomplished in silence until they reached the big old riverside house which housed several large apartments on the floors below the attic flat which had been home to Saskia until recently. She led the way up three flights of stairs and unlocked the door, to find the flat in darkness.

'Come in, then,' she said briskly, turning on lights.

Luke followed her inside, his eyes drawn to her unpacked suitcases behind the sofa.

'Please sit down,' she said politely, taking off her raincoat. She waved him to an armchair and perched on the arm of the sofa. 'What did you want to discuss?'

'The possibility of your coming back to the house.' He stared down at his shoes. 'I admit I was wrong. I admit to jumping to conclusions which sent you storming off. So I'm here to make a proper apology and suggest we start again, on a different basis. I could even charge you rent, if you prefer it that way.'

'And still run the risk of having my every pleasantry looked on as suspect?' she asked scornfully. 'No way!'

'You know perfectly well that would never happen again.' He glared at her. 'You've made it perfectly clear I'm the last man you want to marry. I suppose I should be grateful you consented to make love with me.'

She glared back, pushing damp hair back from the face she knew very well looked pale and tired. 'Are you seeking praise for your sexual prowess?'

'No,' he snapped. 'I thought we were making love, not just having sex.'

Saskia's face flushed scarlet, then paled so suddenly she felt sick, and she slid down onto the sofa cushions abruptly. 'I'm very tired, Luke. You've had your say. The answer's no. So go now, please. I'd like a bath before Carol comes home.'

'I haven't had my say,' he said with quiet violence, and rose to his feet, overpowering in the small room. 'I've got an alternative suggestion.' He breathed in deeply, his face blank as a mask. 'We could get married.'

'What?' She stared at him in such utter astonishment that dark colour rose in his face. 'Why?' she said, mystified.

He shrugged. 'I—want you. So if that's what it takes to have you back I'll marry you.'

'Are you *serious*?'

'Is it the kind of thing one jokes about?'

Green eyes glared into green, and at last Saskia shook her head and looked away. 'Since you make it sound like the last thing in the world you really want, I certainly don't find it funny,' she muttered.

With a smothered curse Luke jerked her into his arms, holding her cruelly tight as she struggled involuntarily to be free. 'Oh, I want you, Sassy. If you need convincing,' he said through his teeth, 'I'll oblige with the greatest of pleasure.' He smothered her protests with a vanquishing kiss, an arm like an iron bar crushing her ribs as his free hand unbuttoned her jacket to gain access to the curves below.

Saskia began to fight in earnest, uttering choked sounds of protest as she fought to get free, but Luke was not only angry, he was now inflamed by the scent and feel of her, the frantic opposition only hardening his resolve to get his way. He swung her up in his arms, then stood stock-still at the sight of the astounded young woman standing in the open doorway.

'Goodness,' said Carol Parker in breathless embarrassment. 'I'm frightfully sorry. Don't mind me. I'll just—' With a nervous laugh she dived for the bedroom and closed the door.

Deathly pale now, Luke set Saskia on her feet, and with shaking hands she tried to re-button her shirt.

'I apologise. Again,' said Luke, and moved to help her, but she dodged away.

'Don't touch me!'

'Saskia—' he began, but she held up a trembling hand.

'If you're capable of any shred of feeling for me, Luke, just go. Please.' Her voice cracked on the last word, and in silence he brushed past her and went out through the door Carol had left open.

Saskia slumped down in a heap on the sofa and began to cry—bitter, racking sobs that brought Carol running from the other room to hold her close in comfort and to apologise volubly for the interruption.

After a while Saskia's sense of proportion returned, and she was able to manage a watery smile. 'Not your fault, Carol. Actually, I'm grateful. Otherwise I might have done something really idiotic.'

'Like letting that gorgeous man have his wicked way?' Carol handed her a wad of tissues. 'Who in the world *was* it?'

'Luke Armytage,' said Saskia, blowing her nose prosaically.

'Your *stepbrother*?' Carol stared at her with eyes like blue saucers.

'We're not actually related.' Saskia drew in a big, shaky breath, and pushed back her hair. 'In fact we've been having a bit of a fling lately.'

'Now let me get this straight,' said Carol, subsiding cross-legged onto the floor. 'Does "a bit of a fling" mean things carnal? In the old days you once told me that leaping in and out of beds was not your cup of tea.'

'It still isn't, in the plural.'

'But Luke's bed is different?'

Saskia nodded dumbly.

'So why were you fighting him tooth and nail?'

'He asked me to marry him.'

Carol stared blankly. 'I don't get it. Look, Saskia, have you lost your marbles?' She grinned widely. 'But if the gentleman is really set on a wife and you don't fancy it, could you point him in *my* direction, please? I wouldn't fight him off, believe me.'

'No chance,' said Saskia firmly, and reached for her handbag. She took the newspaper cutting out and gave it to Carol. 'Luke thinks I did this to push him into it. So I walked out.'

Carol studied the item with interest. 'Who was responsible for this, then?'

'Francis Lawford, in a roundabout way.'

'Ah, yes. I'd forgotten Francis. And, by the look of things when I came in, so had you. Is

Luke right? About the marriage bit? *Is* that the only way you'll go back to him?'

'Of course not,' said Saskia hotly. 'I can't forgive him for even thinking that.'

'Oh, dear, oh, dear.' Carol got up to pat Saskia's bowed, dishevelled head. 'Go and have a bath, then I'll make you my famed beans on toast, or I could defrost something.'

Saskia was feeling rather better by the time she was settled for the night on the pull-out sofa, then she shot upright again as the buzzer rang on the intercom. Carol came running from the bedroom, exclaiming at the cheek of someone calling round at that time of night. She answered it, then eyed Saskia unhappily.

'It's Luke.'

Saskia jumped to her feet, but Carol waved her back.

'Yes, all right,' she said into the intercom. 'I'll come down.' She put the receiver back. 'He's brought something for you, but insists that I, not you, go down to collect it. Flowers, I expect.'

Saskia stared at her friend blankly. 'Why doesn't he want me to go down to collect them, then?'

Carol shrugged and unlocked the door. 'Only one way to find out.'

Saskia waited, tense, until her friend came back a few minutes later, carrying a large carrier bag instead of the expected flowers.

'He brought this for you,' said Carol, looking deeply uncomfortable. 'Said you left it behind.'

The bag provided Saskia with the final, crowning touch to her day. Inside was the Valentino dress.

Saskia went straight to Paddington on the Saturday morning, rang her mother from the train and found Sam Armytage waiting for her at the station when she arrived at Oxford.

Saskia flew into his arms and he hugged her close, then took charge of her hold-all and ushered her outside to the car for a careful drive home through foggy streets while he talked about the twins and his students, and everything under the sun other than Luke.

When she arrived home, Marina was waiting with another hug, and exclamations over her daughter's look of exhaustion. But Saskia assured her mother that she wasn't ill, despite the London pallor, and blamed her frayed appearance on the slave-driving of Charles Harrison.

The twins were having a nap, and after a cautious peep round their door to look at the identical, angelic faces, Saskia changed her travelling clothes for jeans and a sweater, and went downstairs to share lunch with Sam and Marina. She made a rather better job of eating it than any other meal she'd attempted in recent memory as they discussed her new venture into the world of antiques.

'Luke's coming down tonight,' said Marina as they took coffee into the small sitting room. 'Now, don't look like that, Saskia. I know you two are daggers drawn again, but you can just behave yourselves for a day and be civilised, since it's Sam's birthday tomorrow.'

'My sixtieth, too,' said Sam gloomily. 'I need cheering up.'

Saskia swallowed down scalding coffee in one draught and held out her cup for more. 'Of course,' she said valiantly. 'It makes no difference to me.'

Which was such a downright lie Marina smiled in compassion and changed the subject.

'What time did he say he was coming?' said Sam to his wife at one stage.

'Whenever he could get away.'

From what, or from whom? thought her daughter. She should have known Luke would come for Sam's birthday, of course. She'd hoped he would, if she was honest. The past three days had been hard to bear, always hoping he'd ring, or appear again to collect her when she finished work. For the moment she would relax. Just enjoy being home.

The three of them spent the rest of the day catching up on each other's news, all except the one item of news uppermost in the minds of all three. But no one made any more reference to the break between Luke and Saskia, or the reason for it. And after dinner Sam switched on the television to catch up on the news, followed by a weather forecast which confirmed that the southern half of Britain was shrouded in dense fog.

Afterwards, no one having commented on the fact that Luke was driving down from London in such bad weather, they settled down to watch the first instalment of a serial by Marina's favourite thriller writer. And not once did Saskia betray that she was listening for a car, nor what self-control it was taking merely to listen for the chimes of the casement clock in the hall rather than keep looking at her watch.

When the instalment was over, Marina remarked on the fact that Luke was bound to be late, discussed the likely identity of the murderer in the play, then sent Sam upstairs to check on his sons while she made tea.

'After which,' she said, yawning, as Saskia poured, 'Sam and I will go to bed, if you don't mind, darling. Luke said not to wait up for him, so I'll try to get some beauty sleep. I want to look my best for Sam's birthday dinner.'

Saskia was quite glad to go to bed herself. Alone in her old room at the top of the house, she could worry about Luke in private. She settled down in bed with a book, her radio on beside her to listen for traffic flashes. News of a minor pile-up on one of the motorways filled her with terror, but this abated slightly as the presenter reported no fatalities and advised everyone driving out there to slow down and take more care. She tried to concentrate on her book, but without success, shifting restlessly in the bed as she listened to the relentless chimes of the clock marking the passage of time.

At one point she fell into an uneasy doze, then jerked awake and peered at her watch. Two in the morning! She slid out of bed, pulled on her dressing gown and ran down to Luke's room, her blood running cold at the sight of the empty bed. Where in heaven's name *are* you, Luke? she thought in silent anguish. She would ring the police. Saskia stole downstairs in the dark to avoid disturbing the household, then saw a strip of light showing below the kitchen door at the back of the hall.

She tiptoed across to open it, then sagged against the lintel in overwhelming relief. Luke, in all the glory of dinner jacket and black tie, was sitting at the kitchen table with a mug of coffee and the evening paper. He jumped to his feet at the sight of her, unguarded delight in his eyes.

'Saskia!'

Without a word she flung herself across the room, and Luke seized her in his arms and smothered her question with a kiss which made it superfluous. Wherever he'd been, or however late he was, he was here now—in the flesh. She sent up a silent prayer of thanks for it as the kiss lengthened and deepened, and quickly changed from simple thanksgiving to an urgency which threatened to overwhelm them both, and Luke moved his mouth across her cheek to discover tears.

'Don't! Don't cry, Sassy,' he commanded hoarsely.

At which she pulled away, her wet eyes accusing. 'Where the hell have you *been*?' she demanded. 'I've been going out of my mind. I came down to ring the police.'

'Is that true?' He gave her a smile of deep gratification, then eyed her bare feet in disapproval, and picked her up to perch her on the table.

'I've been to a vintners' dinner in Oxford,' he informed her. 'Didn't Marina say?'

'No, she didn't!' said Saskia indignantly. 'I thought you were driving down from London. Mother told me you'd be late and that she wasn't required to wait up for you, so she went off to bed with Sam relatively early.'

'As anyone with three-year-old twins is likely to do, Sassy,' he said with a grin. 'If she let you think I was driving from London through this fog I think your clever mother was conducting an experiment, don't you?'

'You're probably right,' said Saskia wrathfully. 'I shall have something to say to her in the morning!'

'How about thank you?' he suggested, then picked her up again and walked towards the door, switching out the light as he went. 'I'm certainly grateful.'

'What are you doing?' she gasped in his ear.

'Finding somewhere more comfortable.' He went into the morning room, nudging the door closed behind them, then sat down with her on the sofa in the faint glow of the street light filtering through the curtains. 'Now,' he said purposefully, shifting her more comfortably, 'while we have privacy, let's talk, Sassy.'

'What about?'

'Let's continue the conversation we were having when your friend arrived last night.'

'We weren't having a conversation, Luke. You had just picked me up—'

'I've just done that bit, so we may as well go on from there,' he said firmly. 'There's absolutely no point in trying to make out you don't care, Sassy, because a minute or so ago you proved beyond doubt that you do.'

She nodded. 'Which is why I was so mad when you suspected me of trying to force your hand. On the subject of marriage,' she added, just to make things clear.

'You weren't very keen to listen the other night when I came to make amends,' he pointed out.

'Did you expect me to be?'

'I hoped. I just didn't put it over very persuasively.'

'That's an understatement.' Saskia began to giggle, and stifled it against his chest.

'What's so funny?'

'Carol. She had a very interesting evening, from the time she walked in on us to the time you reappeared later with coals of fire in the shape of my beautiful dress.'

'It was in the car. So I turned round at some stage on the way home and brought it back. I knew what I was doing, but I was angry,' he admitted gruffly.

'I know you were. It was a very effective last word, Lucius Armytage. I cried myself to sleep afterwards.'

Luke stared down into her tear-stained face, and let out a deep sigh. 'In which case shall we stop making such a mess of things and start again?' He sat her upright so he could take off his jacket, then pulled her down with him until they were lying full-length together on the comfortable old sofa.

Saskia burrowed closer. 'Yes. But no more marriage proposals, please.'

He stiffened, then forced himself to relax. 'What, then?'

'Could we just live together for a while? I could contribute—'

'Contribute what, precisely?' he demanded.

'Some furniture for the house. I appreciate how expensive—'

The rest of her words were lost against Luke's mouth, and it was some time before he raised his head. 'Saskia, there are several reasons why my house is a bit empty. First of all some basic work had to be done—roof repairs, sanding the floors and so on—most of which was completed while I was on my travels. Those same travels were part of the reason why I haven't bought more furniture. But after I met you in Italy I decided to wait until you helped me choose.'

'Really?' Saskia stared into the intent face so close to hers. 'I thought maybe the money was a problem.'

'Not for a few tables and chairs, Sassy.' He grinned. 'I'm pretty successful at what I do, you know.'

'Very. At *everything* you do,' she said fervently, and wriggled closer.

Luke drew in a deep, unsteady breath and held her still. 'And my grandmother left me some money. Not a vast amount, but good to have behind me. I used some of it to start up the mail-order part of the business, but most of it is invested for such future programmes as furnishing my house and other requirements I shall leave unspecified for the moment.'

'What requirements?' she demanded.

Instead of answering, Luke began to kiss her again, and Saskia responded with such uninhibited enthusiasm that conversation flagged for some time, the need for physical contact greater than the need to talk. For now, even though kissing and caressing was as much as they could allow themselves in the circumstances, it was enough to solace them both for the misery of the past three days. Neither saw the door open a crack, then close again silently, and it was a long time before Saskia remembered her former question.

'What other things are you saving for, Luke?'

'School fees.'

Saskia buried her head against his chest to stifle her laughter. When she raised her head at last he was smiling down at her smugly.

'Isn't that jumping the gun a bit?' She sobered. 'Unless—'

'No unless about it. Whether you marry me or not I want my children to be yours too, Saskia. I love you. It came as a surprise when I found out, I admit, but love you I do, until death us do part, married or not.'

Saskia threw her arms round his neck, tearful again as she kissed him with unrestrained fervour. She drew back, looking him in the eye. 'Then in that case could we perhaps rescue me from my lie?'

'And get engaged?'

She nodded, rubbing her cheek against his. 'No announcement, or anything like that. This is just for us. And Sam and Mother. I just want a ring of some kind.'

'Whatever kind you want,' he said promptly, and got up reluctantly, pulling her to her feet. 'Come on, my darling, time for bed—or the twins might come down and find us.'

'Let's hope we don't meet them on the stairs!'

Luke resumed his jacket and put an arm round her as they crossed the hall to climb the two flights of stairs to her room.

'I wish I could sleep here with you,' he said, closing the door behind him.

'From tomorrow night we shall share a bed every night. If you want. I hope you do. Which reminds me,' she said, chuckling. 'I'd better get in touch with Carol in the morning and tell her she's out of luck.'

'Because she's losing you for a flatmate?'

'No. Because I want you for myself after all. She was very impressed with all that caveman stuff she walked in on—said if I didn't want you I might pass you on to her.'

'Don't I get a say in it?' he demanded irefully.

'None at all. You're mine!'

There was silence for a moment as the words hung in the air between them.

'Are you actually admitting,' he said with care, 'that you love me, Sassy?'

'Of course I am. It may have taken the en- counter in the bathroom at the villa to remove the blinkers from *your* eyes, Lucius Armytage—' Saskia gave him a smile as crooked as his '—but I've loved you all my adult life. Until you walked in on me in Italy nothing would have made me admit it. But from the first day Sam introduced you to us it took just one look for me to—' She broke off as they heard a tap on the door.

'Can I come in? Are you decent?' called Marina softly.

'Yes, on both counts,' said Luke. He opened the door, and bent to kiss Marina's cheek. 'Anything wrong?'

Marina looked from her dishevelled, radiant daughter to her tall, grinning stepson and heaved a great sigh of relief. 'For the moment, nothing in the entire world.' She smiled in delight. 'How about coming down to our room for a glass of champagne? Sam's awake and wants to celebrate. His birthday, for starters. Any other suggestions?'